I0607304

The Bachelor's Agenda

by

Kathye Quick

Bachelors Three, Book 3

This is a work of fiction. Names, characters, places, and incidents are either the product of the author's imagination or are used fictitiously, and any resemblance to actual persons living or dead, business establishments, events, or locales, is entirely coincidental.

The Bachelor's Agenda

COPYRIGHT © 2020 by Kathryn Quick

All rights reserved. No part of this book may be used or reproduced in any manner whatsoever without written permission of the author or The Wild Rose Press, Inc. except in the case of brief quotations embodied in critical articles or reviews.
Contact Information: info@thewildrosepress.com

Cover Art by *Rae Monet, Inc. Design*

The Wild Rose Press, Inc.
PO Box 708
Adams Basin, NY 14410-0708
Visit us at www.thewildrosepress.com

Publishing History
First Sweetheart Rose Edition, 2020
Trade Paperback ISBN 978-1-5092-3189-8
Digital ISBN 978-1-5092-3190-4

Bachelors Three, Book 3
Published in the United States of America

He loosened his tie and peeled off his suit jacket. After neatly folding the coat, he laid it atop the closest file cabinet. He turned and drew down his brows.

Kate had not moved. She stood with arms folded across her chest.

"Was it something I said?"

For a second, she hesitated before the words spilled from her mouth. "Not yet, but I expect soon."

His dark eyes narrowed. "I think we've had a bit of a misunderstanding."

"For you." The heat of anger snaked through her. "I might not be very politically savvy, but I do watch the occasional news story. Let's clear the air, shall we? I don't want to be an intern and move into an apartment a few blocks from yours in Washington." Her finger stabbed the air with each word. "I don't want to be your assistant, your go-fer, or your side chick. I like my job here just fine, so no funny stuff. Get me?"

"I see," Lance said after a moment's hesitation. He gave her a somber nod.

Kate lifted her chin, and her lips twisted in a satisfied smirk. "Glad we understand each other."

Two creases appeared on Lance's brow. "May I ask what you do for a living to make you so passionate?"

What did she do? She couldn't tell him she was a reporter. She blurted out the first thing coming to mind. "I sell johnny ads."

Praise for Kathye Quick and...

***SOLID GOLD BACHELOR*:**
"Carly and Shane have a shattered past that is about to become the present."

~*Brenda M., (4 Stars)*

~*~

***BACHELOR.COM*:**
"Snappy dialogue won me over immediately. I could not stop turning the pages."

~*Kat Henry Dorn, award winning author*

~*~

"If you've never read a Kathryn Quick book, you are in for a treat."

~*Christine Bush, Montlake Romance author*

~*~

Kathryn Quick is:
National Readers Choice Finalist
Winner of two Reviewers Choice Awards
Internationally selling author
Library Journal Holiday Choice Award Author
Amazon top 100 Authors - Montlake Sweet Romance

Dedication

For Mom and Joey

Chapter One

"Kate! Get in here now!"

From her cubicle at the rear of the small office and over the din of telephones and copy machines, Kate barely heard Peter Gartman bellow. She glanced over her reading glasses at the only real office on the floor. He wasn't at the door. *Yet.* About a half hour remained until her story was due in his outbox, so a missed deadline wasn't why her boss screamed her name. Five minutes and she'd be done with the article. He could wait.

Katherine Anne Stapleton, Kate to most people, caught the journalism and writing bug as editor-in-chief of her high school newspaper. Her writing success continued through college, but, after graduation, she found a whole lot less welcoming community. Now, as contributor to an online tabloid called *The Analytical*, she was at the mercy of a neurotic boss and a whole lot of other journalists and writers fighting to break into the mainstream market.

Five years later and despite thousands of likes on her social media page, none of the interviews she had with print media or a few magazine companies translated into any 'you're-hireds.' But the job paid the bills, and her nights meant a lot of hunting for something better on the internet or in local papers. Though not totally dissuaded, she did want something to happen soon.

"Kate. Now." The call came again.

Kate heard the wheels of her coworker's chair slide.

A second later, Susan, a chatty brunette, appeared from behind the right partition.

"That's two," she said. "You have one more shout before Gartman comes out. I beg you. Go in there and save the rest of us." She scooted her chair backward, her hands assuming the pleading position. "I'll buy dinner tonight. Just don't let him come out here."

Kate dropped her head, her hair covering the frown on her face. She reached for the hair elastic around her wrist and forced the unruly curls into a ponytail. "I wonder what he has in mind for me now." She lifted her head and trained her gaze on her roommate. "I feel like Italian. *Taste of Italy* at seven. Meet you there."

Susan mouthed a thank-you and scooted her chair into place.

Smacking her hands on her thighs, Kate lifted her head. "On my way, boss." As she walked to his office, she swore she heard faint applause. At the door, she stopped and took a deep breath before stepping inside. "What's so pressing, Mr. Gartman?"

He stood with arms folded across his chest, staring at the laptop on his desk. Gartman gestured with his right hand. "Will you look at this guy?" He spun the laptop toward her.

Kate heard music and voices as she circled around his desk. As Kate watched the live feed, she collided with a pair of brown-gold eyes set between dark spiky lashes on the face of New Jersey Senator Lance Michaels. Her jaw dropped as she let out a breath. *Holy moly. This guy is gorgeous.* For a moment, she nearly forgot where she was.

The camera shot pulled back, and her gaze fixed on the senator like radar on a target as he waved and walked to the stage. What woman wouldn't recognize him? Six years earlier at thirty-two, Lance Michaels made history by becoming the youngest candidate to win election to the United States Senate. In doing so he also instantly became the focus of the mainstream media and the pin-up boy for women voters in New Jersey. She watched the tall, thin, and toned senator with the physique of a natural athlete approach the dais and imagined he would still easily cause a stir at every campaign stop. For some reason, she remembered being told the average age of a U.S. Senator was sixty-five.

In the months immediately after his election, the mainstream press corps zeroed in on his youth and inexperience, joking he could easily find another career by looks alone should his rookie term be as ineffective as most media outlets predicted. But in the ensuing six years since his historic victory, he proved everyone wrong and carved his place in Washington politics.

Though, Kate admitted she had paid little attention. After all, she worked for an online tabloid whose readership cared more about which celebrity was taken up in UFO, rather than balanced budgets and the everyday opinionated bickering on Capitol Hill.

The camera shot followed the senator's long strides to the stage. He was taller than most of those in the crowd applauding and making a path for him. His wide shoulders and lean hips fit perfectly into the dark suit he wore, probably ordered from whatever men's wear designer was trendy in D.C. these days. Kate felt her mouth drop open when he reached the podium and his rich dark voice wrapped around her when he acknowledged those still applauding. She gave her head a quick shake to fend off her curious reaction but had to admit he wasn't hard on the eyes. Maybe she should have paid more attention to politics.

Gartman frowned, his eyes narrowing. "Not you, too."

"Not me too what?"

He gestured to an empty chair and pointed to the laptop screen. "You aren't falling for the hype, are you? Because if you are, you might as well leave now and send in Benson. I can give him this assignment."

As she settled into the chair, she felt a sourness rise in her throat at the mention of Benson's name. She knew Gartman considered Jim Benson his best investigative reporter, if the term applied to the literary license and wild theories Benson wove into his reporting instead of facts and actual coverage. She was very curious why Gartman would offer her an assignment over his ace and was more than a bit suspicious about what devious angle swirled in Gartman's head. But she was not about to pass on this assignment before she heard him out.

"No so fast. I'm interested." She slid her arms onto the desk, leaned forward, and fixed her gaze on him as she sat. "What are you looking for?"

"Dirt," Gartman said.

"Dirt?" she repeated, brow wrinkling.

Gartman nodded and shut the laptop. "And plenty of it. I want enough to last all campaign season."

Kate imagined a few juicy headlines. "Shouldn't be a problem. Some level of conniving is always happening in D.C."

He pulled a file folder out of a desk drawer and slid it across his desk. "I've been doing legwork on the guy and know what I found?"

She shook her head and stopped the folder from landing on the floor.

"Open it."

When she did, all she found was a blank piece of paper. Her eyes narrowed as her thoughts raced to make sense of the situation. She held it up. "And this is?"

"The sum total of our boy's questionable deeds over the last six years."

Again, she looked at the paper. "It's empty."

"Yep, I found nothing." Gartman leaned forward and frowned. "A big bowl of zilch. Now I ask you, what politician doesn't have a skeleton or two in the closet or a back-door deal that would further his career or help a friend? Couldn't find a darn thing. No kick-back charges, no pay-to-play gifts, no favors promised. Nothing." His eyes narrowed. "This guy has to be hiding something. I can feel it." He sat back and cupped his hands around his head. "We all have secrets. I want his."

Kate angled the chair and crossed her long legs. She tossed the file folder into the garbage can. "No reports of affairs with interns?"

"Not that I can find."

"You sure he had no covert negotiations with foreign governments?"

"None."

Mentally running through old news stories of previous scandals, she threw out another option. "Rumors of taking gifts from special interest groups?"

Gartman shook his head.

Visions of reporting for one of the major TV networks or a possible syndicated byline in a national newspaper formed in Kate's head. She stood and extended her hand. "No one is that perfect. I'm in."

****

Lance Michaels read the final line of his speech from the teleprompter before looking over the sea of supporters who attended his first major fundraiser since announcing his intent to run for re-election as one of the two senators from the State of New Jersey. He swiveled his gaze right to left as the crowd stood like a human wave in an athletic stadium. Both humbled and excited with the thought of another six-year round of public service in one of the toughest arenas in the country, determination bubbled inside him. He accomplished a lot but also knew he left a lot undone due to partisan bickering. While he did not want to be a career politician, another term would allow him to finish what he started.

He leaned toward the microphone on the podium. "Thank you all for your past support, and I hope I can count on you in the months to come." He raised a hand and acknowledged the cheers and shouts before turning to leave the stage.

A large man in a dark suit with a wire coiling from under his jacket connecting to an earpiece stepped forward. "Ready to go, sir?"

"You bet, Jack." He waited until Jack and two other members of the security team made a pathway toward the door. As he edged his way forward, he was again grateful Jack Turner was not only lead on the team but also a trusted friend.

Outside, on the way to the car, Lance shook hands outstretched between bodies lining the pathway. A few people shouted compliments, and others held out cell phones to catch a quick photo Lance surmised would shortly appear on social media. At the car, he stopped for a mere second to offer one final wave before ducking inside the back seat. The door closed.

A moment later, the driver exited, and Jack slid behind the wheel. The secondary security team got into the car behind. With the horn beeping a warning, Jack steered the idling car away from the curb.

Lance glanced out the rear window. Some people stood in the middle of the street, waving, but most were dispersing. After letting out a long breath, he settled into the seat and loosened his tie. "So, it begins, Jack. Ready for another political silly season?"

Jack Turner, the senior security officer, nodded. "Ready as I'll ever be." He removed his earpiece. "You should be fine."

Lance waved to some lingering supporters as the car pulled out of the driveway, and, with a single blink of headlights of the following car, the secondary team broke off. "Not so sure. I've got some tough competition from the assemblyman from South Jersey. I'll have a battle on my hands this time."

"Possibly, sir." Jack tapped a forefinger on the steering wheel. "I can get a team digging into his record over his last three terms in the New Jersey Legislature and see if any red flags surface in a matter of days."

Lance waved off the remark with a firm slash of his hand in the air. "I know that look, Jack. While I do appreciate your vigilance, we are not stooping to any kind of low. You know what I say, when you sling mud…"

"…some always blows back on you," Jack finished. "But taking the high road in this campaign doesn't mean your opponent is looking into your background as we speak."

Lance laughed. "Then I suppose I had better make sure I only wear my dark suits."

"Sir?"

"For the mud."

"Are you telling me in a roundabout way you have a checkered past?" Jack asked.

"Boring as white bread," Lance admitted. "Twelve years in Catholic School, four more at Notre Dame, and an ultra-conservative nature does not leave much time for sin."

Jack snickered. "One might conclude from the list you might be a…."

Lance held up a hand. "I said boring, not dead."

Both men laughed.

"I know D.C. can be tough, sir, especially during campaign season."

"Tougher than I originally thought."

"You're doing well."

Expecting more Lance waited for a moment. "You think so?"

Jack nodded. "Yes, sir, I do. You don't nibble when baited, and you stay on point during a conversation or debate." He kept nodding while he spoke. "Mark of a seasoned politician."

"That's something I never want to become," Lance said with a firm shake of his head. He didn't want to blurt out how he really felt. While he did enjoy being a senator, the slow-walk of Washington politics interfered with his eagerness to advance the agenda he promised his supporters. Getting enough support for a project through committee took ten times longer than expected, and the deals made to collect the votes needed to get a bill out of committee left a sour taste in his mouth at times. Still, he was not ready to give up. He wanted to make a difference and believed in the democratic process upon which America had been built.

"What I need to pay your security team during the campaign would seem obscene to most." He forced a laugh that sounded false to his own ears. "Keeping the whack-a-doodles who disagree with my politics at bay leaves me little money to wine and dine anyone." The notion of spending another six years cautious of people getting close raced across Lance's mind. Though he accepted the sacrifice of privacy in exchange for duty to country when he was elected, more and more he missed the freedom of being a private citizen. At the end of the day he would like someone to talk with besides the press, lobbyists, or supporters.

Although the life of a United States Senator did bring a sense of fame and glory, duty to country had a darker side. With no lack of individuals always looking for a way to penetrate inner circles or secure a lucrative government contract, he developed a persistent sense of wariness, especially of someone getting too close too soon. Though more and more he considered missing out on a normal life for another six years in office a high price to pay, he was resolute about finishing the agenda he began in exchange for what he hoped would be a more prosperous nation with citizens who felt safer.

"You know the President's security detail is paid for by the American people."

Jack's voice brought Lance from his reverie. "You might not be able to work for me. The Secret Service has a pecking order for assignments."

"Even so, you'd be good at the job, sir." Jack made steady eye contact. "Real good."

"Well, that's one of us who thinks so." In his mind he was still a rookie at the political game. Thinking any farther than another term in the Senate overwhelmed him with the amount of time and energy he would need. Maybe in another ten years. For now, he had a lot to learn. "I think the voters would agree."

Lance shook his head. "Though the most powerful position on the planet, the office of the President is afforded more responsibility and even less freedom than I have now." His words mirrored his thoughts. He wasn't ready. "At the moment I don't want another job. I am still learning the one I have."

Jack turned and briefly captured Lance's gaze. "Something to be said about on-the-job training."

"Not when you possibly affect the future of the world with every decision made." As the car headed toward the highway, streetlights gave way to rural darkness. Lance reached up, opened the sun roof, and pointed to the sky. He paused for a moment. Such a vast marvel overhead. Such possibilities awaiting the courageous. The sight reminded him of the person he wished to be in the Senate if he had the courage to explore the unknown like an astronaut shooting into space and not knowing what he would find. "See the stars?"

Jack looked at the night sky. "I do, sir."

"If the city lights are too bright, you can't see them. You have to go somewhere devoid of artificial light, like a calm quiet place where you can lay down in a pick-up bed or on a soft mound of grass, and just enjoy the moment." He snickered. "Can you appreciate the irony? Washington is like that scenario. Only after you go to a dark place can you see the light."

Again, Jack looked up at the star-studded sky. "Well, sir, maybe you should take a picture now, because for the next few months, not many quiet moments will crop up. I suspect you'll be missing that view."

Lance nodded. Though the battle for another term officially began with his primary win in June, the intense part of the campaign started in September and would run right up to Election Day in November. As the whine of the sunroof closing echoed in the car, he watched the stars gradually disappear. A sign, he decided. He knew exactly what lay ahead. No time for relaxing or star gazing would be available until the winner of his senate seat was decided in about ninety days.

****

Kate wove through tables of diners at a popular eatery in the next town over like she maneuvered an obstacle course. "Sorry I'm late," she said when the hostess led her to a back booth. She guessed Susan had been waiting for almost thirty minutes, but the delay could not be helped.

Susan accepted the apology with a nod. "I figured you might be held up. You were still in the boss' office when I left." She sipped her red wine. "Big assignment?"

"The biggest." Kate hung her coat on the hook outside the booth and stashed a full tote bag on the bench seat. She cleared a spot on the table in front of her and removed items from the tote bag. "Could be the story of a lifetime. If I can pull off this exclusive, I could be actually out of tabloid journalism."

Susan grabbed the senator's head shot. "I am guessing the assignment has something to do with Senator McDreamy." She winked, a big smile emerging. "I'd change political parties for a run at this guy."

"Forget the election." Kate snatched back the photo. "I have no intention of writing ten inches of copy about how the voting-age women in New Jersey swoon over this guy. I need a better story." She shuffled through the newspaper clippings. "Somewhere in here is the senator's Achilles Heel, and I'll find it."

"Wouldn't using a computer and a great search engine be more efficient?"

"Maybe, but you get the real stuff when you do the legwork and actually talk to people." Kate spread the series of stories across the table just as the server approached. She barely looked up as she arranged the clippings on the table and gestured to Susan. "I'll have whatever she's having."

"Burgers and fries." Susan glanced at the paper-covered table. "On very small plates."

Kate acknowledged the disparagement in her friend's tone with a mouthed *ha-ha* and looked through the copy. "I could not find anything." She picked up a stack of papers and handed them to Susan. "Here. Let me know what you think."

After a few minutes of silence while Susan read through the mound she shrugged. "I think the man is a saint." She slid the papers back to Kate. "You couldn't find anything because nothing is there to find. At least, not in any of these stories."

Kate's breath left in a loud whoosh, and she slumped back in the seat. "I know. That's what is so infuriating." She straightened. "Unless…"

"I know that look. The gears are turning in your head. What's the angle?"

"Unless the senator has been very carefully hiding a dark secret."

Susan shook her head. "Not in the day and age of social media. If he has a spurned girlfriend, an ex-wife or something, I'm sure we'd know already."

"Maybe a love child?"

"Doubt it. Nobody keeps babies from past relationships with an icon a secret these days."

Kate frowned. She put an elbow on the table and leaned her chin on her cupped hand. "But something has to have happened. We've all done things we regret." She turned her head toward the head shot leaning against the pepper mill. "He must have a few regrets, too."

"None the media found." She cleared a spot on the table as the server brought their dinner.

"Until now." Kate felt excitement bubble inside her. "Maybe he is so corrupt a crime boss protects his reputation in order to call in a huge favor after the senator rises through the ranks." She smacked a hand on the tabletop. "I've heard some people wait *years* for a plan to work."

"Doubt it. Social media." Susan wrinkled her nose. "Someone would have found out by now, and the story would be among these articles or posted on the web." She drew a slightly burnt French fry across the mound of ketchup on her plate. "The main stream political media is relentless. News, fake news, whatever it took, if Senator Michaels sinned, we'd know."

Mentally, she quickly ran through some contacts she still maintained from her days as a stringer. Maybe one of them heard or knew something. "Not if Senator Michaels paid someone to keep quiet."

Susan laughed. "*Especially* if Senator Michaels paid someone to keep quiet. You know what they say about everyone wanting their fifteen minutes of fame. Someone would have come forward by now."

Kate pictured a crush of reporters surrounding the senator and shoving microphones in his face after she broke the story she was sure she would write. The small smile that began quickly faded. "Capitol Hill doesn't play by the same rules as normal people do. Someone could have something big on Senator Michaels and is keeping quiet for now."

"Like what?"

"I don't know. Maybe he brokered a high-powered job on Capitol Hill for a family member of a particularly annoying lobbyist." She grabbed her cell phone and entered a few notes on where to start looking. "Global warming is a hot topic. Maybe the senator got someone an inside track on a bill being posted for a vote."

"I thought you hated politics."

Kate snickered. "Until I've got my story, I'm all over the affairs of state."

Susan held up a hand. "Too much drama already. Keep it up, and I'll get indigestion." She gathered the articles on the table and handed them to Kate. "Let's just finish dinner, have another glass of wine, and not talk shop for a while."

As she thought over the suggestion, Kate took a deep breath and held it until her lungs burned. She let out the breath slowly. "Okay, but enjoy this little moment of calm while we have it."

"We?" Susan raised an eyebrow. "I write on tech stuff, not scandals."

Kate nodded and thrust a forefinger toward her. "I am getting this story, and you will be helping me."

****

Later in the day, Kate sat cross-legged on her bed with articles about Senator Michaels spread across the quilt her grandmother made. She tapped her fingernails on her chin. She worked for some tough editors, some brilliant editors, and even one or two alcoholic editors, all of whom could take a kernel of an idea, turn it upside down and backwards, and come out with a good second page. But over the course of her not-so-amazing career in journalism, she had never worked for an editor like Gartman. God willing, if this assignment worked out, she never would again.

Her immediate plan was to dog the senator until she got what she needed and turn what she found into front page news. Then she'd take one of the high-powered jobs she would be offered, leaving Gartman to figure out what happened.

She was dreaming of a new and very sizable income when the ring tone she assigned to Gartman shook her out of plotting her jump from tabloid journalism to mainstream media. He started talking as soon as she answered. "How do you feel about class reunions?"

Kate furrowed her brow. "Whose?"

"His."

"The senator's?" She heard the front legs of his chair hit the floor and decided he still was at the office. "When?"

"Tomorrow night. I got a tip from one of his staffers he's kicking off his grassroots campaign at his high school class reunion, and you need to start digging for dirt." He slapped his hands together. "Perfect opportunity."

She laughed at the thought. "I'm ten years younger than Senator Michaels, and I went to high school in New Hampshire. How am I supposed to masquerade as a former student of a school I never attended?"

"You'll have to figure out how. I'll text you some details." The call disconnected.

The buzzing of his incoming text began. Gartman's suggestions ranged from seducing the senator to hiring a private investigator to tail him—at her expense of course. She rejected them all. This assignment was hers, and she was a good journalist. She didn't need devious tactics to get the needed details. With no need to keep the text, she hit delete and tossed her phone onto the nightstand.

She walked to the dresser and stared into the large mirror. How could she age ten years in a matter of a few days? After pulling back her hair and piling a loose ponytail on top of her head, she decided she could pull off a more mature look. She'd borrow a knee-length dress from Susan and wear sensible shoes then pray to blend in with the rest of the attendees.

Her mind spun with possible answers to questions that might come up such as why she wasn't in the yearbook and when did she transfer. She was a tabloid reporter and made up a lot of stuff. She could easily invent a character with a quasi-believable background to possibly satisfy even the most ardent alumni. The only risk would be remembering what was said and to whom. She only hoped the attendees would pay more attention to the eminent alumnus rather than someone they didn't remember. A sharp pang of uncertainty momentarily ripped through her. If she didn't pull this off, her job and her reputation were both toast.

Chapter Two

The next evening, Kate stood outside the restaurant and looked at the blue-and-white banner above the door. Ridgemont High School—Twentieth Reunion. A blue mustang accented each side of the words. The mascot, she surmised. She'd better remember the horse and the school colors. High school football jocks allegedly recalled every moment of youthful sports glory. She'd be wise to avoid conversations about game-winning touchdowns or last-minute basketball penalty shots.

She glanced first at the parking lot then the door. The lot was filling but not fast enough. About fifteen minutes earlier, she got behind two couples walking into the reunion but stopped before reaching the check-in table. She'd forgotten about registration until she saw the nametags spread across the long tabletop in front of doors leading to the banquet hall. Ideally, she wanted a group of about ten people keeping the two registrants busy enough for her to grab a blank name tag and slip inside.

Katie Taylor, January transfer student from the Midwest, was the alumni persona she settled upon after inventing two or three other characters. She was confident her new name sounded very common and one easily forgotten over the years, especially when transferring in with only six months left in senior year.

Outside, as she sat on the rock wall lining the landscaping, she looked up at the overcast sky to avoid a few curious looks from passersby. She hoped to be inside when Senator Michaels arrived. Members of his advance team were probably already mingling. Good bodyguards alerted when the public figures arrived.

She planned on sitting at a back table where those not in the popular cliques of high school times would probably gather. Despite not attending her own reunion last year, she made some quick calls over the past few days to friends who had. From them, she got the impression perspectives had not matured with time, and most alumni gravitated to those with whom they had been friends in the past. Jocks still hung with jocks, brainiacs with other intellectuals, and so on. She suspected the same would hold true for this gathering. This post-graduate pecking order would work to her advantage. The deeper she delved into this assignment, the more the challenge stimulated her journalistic intuition.

She didn't know why Gartman gave her the nod over Benson, who was Gartman's golden-child. When she was hired, she hoped to report on corporate insider trading, murder, or drug trafficking, but Gartman gave her shoplifting, ticket scalping, telephone scams, or celebrity social climbing. Over the years, he didn't compliment or criticize her writing, leaving her in a sort of limbo. Now, she had control over her fate. He just might have handed her a lead on government corruption and a way out of the tabloids without even realizing he had.

Five cars eased into the valet parking line, and eight couples emerged and greeted each other as though they were still in high school while the valet collected keys and distributed tags.

The organized chaos created the distraction Kate needed. She donned her brightest smile and stepped behind them.

At the reception table, she waited until the registrants were totally immersed with matching spoken names to those printed on self-stick badges before palming a blank name tag and black felt-tipped pen then moving quickly through the open door. Once inside the banquet room, she scribbled her new name onto the name badge and dropped the pen onto an empty serving tray set near the wall.

As she surveyed the tables, she heard nostalgic music playing, but no one was on the dance floor. Most attendees stood waiting in line at the bar. Near the kitchen sat a table with two seated couples looking totally bored as they stared at the deejay. Perfect. Table twenty nine. She grinned and walked to one of the empty chairs. "Is this seat taken?"

One of the women turned briefly before she resumed staring.

Kate waited for a verbal response but none came. She was in. *Posing as a graduate will be easier than I thought.* She slid out a metal chair and held her smile as she sat. All she had to do now was wait for the senator to make his grand entrance.

****

Lance sat in the back of the extended cab pick-up, his knees almost touching his chest. "Seriously, Jack? This interior is not meant for someone over six foot." He pointed to the junior member of his security team sitting comfortably in the passenger seat. "Why couldn't Sam sit back here?"

As Jack eased the truck down the exit and off the highway, he glanced over his shoulder. "Sir, you know protocol. For your safety, you can't sit in the front."

"You might have to use the Jaws-of-Life to get me out." Lance angled his body and stretched his long legs as much as the space allowed. "Tell me again why we didn't use the limo."

"Bad tranny, sir."

"Nothing else was available?" He looked inside. He hated small, cramped spaces that reminded him of being trapped in the room during committee meetings. No escape until each member had his or her say. He was more a let's-get-going person while career politicians enjoyed the sound of their own voices. In either case, he didn't have a choice. He'd have to get to where he had to be no matter the circumstances. "Not even the SUV with the dent in the fender?"

"No, sir."

Lance shrugged. "So much for political perks." He hopped inside the small rear seat and settled back.

After getting behind the wheel, Jack made eye contact via the rearview mirror. "I didn't know you would take a freebie."

"To be honest, about an hour ago I thought about calling in a favor."

"How so, sir?" Jack asked.

Lance grabbed the edge of the driver's seat and inclined forward. "I was tempted to ask the county party chairman to call and offer my regrets citing a last-minute meeting." He frowned. "I was never a fan of starting my grassroots campaign by using my high school reunion."

Jack laughed. "You won't be campaigning, sir. You'll be having an enjoyable visit with old friends."

"Right. Old friends." Lance snickered. "I haven't seen most of them since graduation. I can count on one hand those I did meet who agreed with my agenda."

"Should make for an interesting evening then."

A muscle ticked along Lance's jaw line. "You never told me who dreamed up this brilliant idea."

Jack smothered a grin. "Does it matter now? Ten minutes and you're on."

"Then today's code word is stimulating." He pointed to his face. "Once I rub my right eye, and you hear me say it, you have five minutes to get me out, or you're fired."

Jack turned on the left blinker and pulled onto a two-lane street heading into town. "Understood, but with three months until the election, if you fire me, I might sell a tell-all story to a newspaper like those stacked on the impulse shelves in the grocery check-out aisle."

Lance sat back. "Not a chance. My life is boring. At the most, your blockbuster story might help sell five more papers than normal." He grinned. "Besides, I can spot a tabloid reporter as soon as I enter a room, so I have nothing to worry about."

****

"He's here!"

The announcement from the bleached blonde at the next table and sounded more like a squeal. Kate turned. "How do you know?"

The blonde pointed. "See those guys at the door with the wires curling alongside their necks from earpieces. They must be Secret Service."

To get a better look, Kate leaned forward. "They aren't Secret Service. I bet they're part of the senator's advance team."

The woman scoffed. "How do you know?"

"Congressional leadership such as the Speaker of the House and Senate President has protection twenty-four-seven. But the rest of Congress only has Secret Service protection when in the Capitol Building." She gestured to the men at either side of the door. "Just because those large men in dark suits are here doesn't mean the senator has arrived."

The woman sat back and looked Kate up and down. "Are you a history teacher or something?"

Kate shook her head. "Just interested. I liked civics class." She saw the woman's forehead wrinkle and suspected she might be in a bit of trouble.

"We didn't have a civics class."

Had she blown her cover already? Beads of perspiration formed between her shoulder blades. "I meant at my old school. I transferred in my senior year."

The woman's frown deepened. "I don't remember anyone coming in then."

Think of something before she pulls out a yearbook. "I was very forgettable back then."

"Where did you say you came from?"

"The Midwest." Kate noticed the woman's half-empty glass and hiked a thumb over her shoulder. "I was about to get some water. Can I get you something from the bar?"

Kate's tablemate quickly finished her drink. "Sure. How about a seven-and-seven?" She handed Kate her glass. "And my husband would probably like another beer."

Kate rose. "Coming up." She headed for the bar and never looked back. If she talked to the woman any longer, she'd be exposed and escorted out, possibly ending her quest to get out of the tabloid business forever. From now on, she'd have to be more careful and less talkative.

****

Jack's pick-up pulled into the reserved parking spot in front of the restaurant. He angled his body and glanced at Lance. "Ready, sir?"

"As ready as I'll ever be." Lance straightened his red tie and noticed people being ushered away from the sidewalk by two men in dark suits. He pointed. "Did they really need the dark glasses?"

"Special optics, sir."

He scowled. "I'm not the President."

"Yet."

The frown deepened. "No jokes until the evening is over."

Jack laughed and stepped out of the truck about the same time Sam opened the passenger door.

Lance squared his shoulders. He really disliked the amount of time campaign season took from doing his job in Washington. The eight weeks between the end of the summer and Election Day set him back double the time. He never knew what deals would be made in his absence or how many he would have to work against. But campaign was a necessary evil if he wanted to return to the Senate, and he already made that choice. Taking a deep breath, Lance exited.

A buzz rose from the crowd, and the inevitable calling began.

"Good luck in November."

"You have my vote, Senator."

"Not mine."

The negative comment was instantly shouted down by more positive remarks.

Glancing toward the opposing voice, Lance smiled. "I respect your right to choose, sir." A spattering of applause rose. As he walked toward the restaurant entrance, he waved and buttoned his suit jacket. There, he paused and turned to Jack. "Game face."

Jack winked. "That's a given, sir."

This was the part of Washington life Lance actually hated. He wanted to work, not campaign, but to accomplish the former, he had to pull off the latter. Before he could let the frustration of the time he wasted shaking hands and kissing babies steal beneath his skin, he pasted on a smile and walked through the front door.

Chapter Three

Kate kept her gaze on the three glasses she held as she moved slowly through the crowd. She was nearly to her seat when the sound of chairs moving and a chorus of voices combined into a racket as a third man with an obvious earpiece moved into position at the main door.

Most of the attendees scrambled to the front and formed a line near the door.

Just as she was about to set the drinks on the table, someone passing on the way to the back of the room bumped her, and she pitched forward. She juggled two glasses upright but not the third. The tumbler hit the floor near her right shoe, and the liquid splashed onto the hem of her dress. She looked down and sighed then looked at the tall man in the dark suit. "That's going to leave a mark."

"Sorry, ma'am." He pulled a neatly folded handkerchief from his inside jacket pocket and held it out. "I'd be happy to pay for the dry cleaning."

Kate swiped at the wet spot. "No need."

"But your dress might be ruined."

Cheering nearly drowned out the man's comment.

She leaned toward him. "It's okay."

Applause echoed, and he looked away, his attention suddenly drawn to commotion at the door. He clasped his hands in front of him. "Can we speak later?"

She followed his gaze and noticed everyone in the room now stood. Rising on tiptoes, she caught a glimpse of the senator. "Sure. I see the guest of honor has arrived."

"Thank you, ma'am."

Kate watched him take a position next to the kitchen door. Back straight and wearing a somber expression, he scrutinized everyone around the senator with eyes that seemed to be on a swivel. His body language told her he didn't care about being conspicuous, so he had to be part of the senator's security team. Maybe she could trade a ruined dress for an introduction. After selecting one of the remaining drinks, she settled into a spot next to him. "I'm Kate."

"Jack," he said without looking.

She took a healthy sip of her drink but barely tasted the liquor. She tipped the glass toward Jack. "Won't get tipsy on this."

Jack said nothing.

Undaunted, she tried another approach. "Pretty exciting having the senator at this reunion."

Jack's head turned to the left, his gaze following the senator as he made his way around the room. "Yes, ma'am."

Kate held the straw between her thumb and forefinger and sipped between words. "If you are with the security team, you don't blend in very well."

"In some situations, standing out is better."

Kate noticed Senator Michaels was roughly two tables into the obligatory greeting of the attendees. "I'd like to meet the senator."

Jack lifted his chin. "Looks like Senator Michaels will be at your table shortly."

"I don't mean like meet on a rope line with a passing handshake." Kate flashed what she hoped was a demure smile. "More like one-on-one."

"I don't think so, ma'am."

"Why not?" Kate felt more disappointed with her dismal approach than with the result. "An introduction is the least you can do after ruining a perfectly good dress."

"The senator is on a very tight schedule." He gestured to her table. "Please."

Kate shrugged and started back to her table. After two steps, she turned. "But you'd make a few more brownie points if you called me miss instead of ma'am." Just as the last word was out, she realized Jack had moved.

"That's a great suggestion. I'll make sure I do, miss."

The deep male voice answering wrapped around Kate like a warm afghan on a cold day. She closed her eyes, and then opened them slowly. She was glad she'd forgotten to add blush to tonight's make-up. The heat of embarrassment scorched her cheeks. "Senator," she whispered through her closing throat. "Nice to meet you."

His gaze briefly moved to her cheeks. "I hope I didn't startle you."

Kate swore she heard him chuckle. "No. Why would you think you had?" She stumbled through her reply.

He looked again at her cheeks.

"A bit warm in here, don't you think, Senator?" Kate fanned her face with a hand. "One would think a place like this would have better air conditioning."

"One would." Lance extended his hand. "And call me Lance. I'm not the formal type."

"Okay." She hesitated. "Lance." *All right. I'm in again.* She leaned toward him. "What should I say now?" She hoped she was the only one who heard his quiet laughter.

"We can start with your name."

"Kate." Her name came out in a feeble squeak. She raised her hand slowly. His smile matched the one reflected in his voice.

"Just Kate?" He raised his eyebrows and took her hand.

Unexpected warmth rose on her skin where he touched her, and she suddenly could not think of one intelligent thing to say. His grip was firm and very commanding. The contact made her think of volcanoes and high-voltage wires or a blazing fire and a hot summer day—everything but the last name she concocted. Her heartbeat raced as she once again looked into the most remarkable eyes she had ever encountered. "Sawyer," she whispered. "Kate Sawyer."

"I thought you said your name was Taylor," one of the women waiting to greet the senator remarked.

For one heart-stopping moment, she thought she had blown her cover. She spun to the woman and shrugged. "I really need to remember to use my maiden name." She turned and faced Lance. "Newly single."

"Fortunate for all the single men," Lance replied.

For a moment, his gaze flickered down to her mouth then back up to her eyes. Kate suddenly realized just how personal and extended the handshake had become. She was here to do a job, not meet a man. She eased free her hand and stepped back. She laughed out a short puff of air and pictured Benson as her ex-husband to get into character. "I don't think the ex would agree." She raised a hand in an exaggerated stay-away motion. "He'd say, 'Watch out, she's loose.' "

Lance grinned. "His loss." His brow creased. "Were we in any classes together?"

"English." Everyone in her real high school had to take four years of English in one form or another before graduation. She hoped the same requirements existed at Ridgemont High. "But I doubt if you would remember me." She laughed. "I was about fifty pounds heavier and had short curly hair and thick glasses." More lies. She prayed she remembered them all.

The crease across his forehead deepened, and he shook his head. "Can't say I do remember you."

Glad she rehearsed answers just for a situation like this, she waved off the remark. "Typical case of forgettable geeks versus the memorable cool kids." She cupped one side of her mouth and lowered her voice. "But now all the cool kids work for the geeks." She saw his brows draw down, as if searching for a comment, and she suspected her attempt at humor drifted right over his head, which was difficult since he was taller than the average person in the room. He stood to the north of six feet she guessed, and she did like tall men. Now, her brow crinkled. *Why did I think of that?*

"I wasn't..." he began

"Oh, I didn't mean you." She flashed her brightest grin which normally got her out of some tight situations. If her ruse worked on the senator, he was a master of disguise because his expression never changed. Time to give the man some room. She nodded. "Well, very nice to meet you, Senator. Good luck with the election."

"Maybe we'll meet again somewhere along the campaign trail," he said.

"I doubt it. I'm not into politics." *Keep lying, Kate, and you'll punch your one-way ticket to hell.*

"A pity." He smiled and stepped toward the next outstretched hand.

Kate didn't have time to ask what he meant as he disappeared in the crush of adoring admirers. She caught brief glimpses of him as the crowd swelled and thinned. If her heartbeat was a barometer for emotion, she was headed straight for confusion over why she reacted so strongly to their very brief meeting. Maybe his confidence caused her gaze to sweep across the throng and locate him, or perhaps she gave him the twice-over to size him up for the eventual takedown.

He turned, caught her staring, and flashed a smile that transformed his face into a picture of pure charm. He did it so effortlessly she wondered how many more votes he would get just by turning up the charisma. Again, he glanced at her, and she noticed his eyes flashed with every bit of candlepower they possessed. When his lids lowered and his eyes crinkled at the corners, his smile made her heartbeat rise. She lowered her gaze and made her way to her table. This evening was not going the way she planned.

****

Out of the corner of his eye, Lance watched Kate, his practiced mind still responding to the questions and the comments of those around him. He met thousands of people during his tenure in politics, but this was the first time when an initial impression felt so strong. Something about Kate intrigued him. He couldn't decide exactly what was different about her, but he was not leaving the reunion until he found out.

He eased his way around the room and toward her table. When he glanced in her direction, he noticed the way the lights played off her hair and imagined the softness of her curls running across the back of his hand. He knew better than to make any such overture in public and resisted the urge to find out. He caught her gaze and nodded.

She wiggled her fingers and turned away.

He smiled and knew the other woman whose hand he shook thought the grin was for her, but the enjoyment on his face was one of irony. Originally, he had no intention of staying at the reunion longer than necessary to greet everyone and begin his grassroots campaign, but now he was in no hurry to leave. A few more tables remained to visit, and then, like a politician delivering a filibuster on the Congress floor, he was not going anywhere for a while.

Jack appeared at his left. "Is the evening getting a bit stimulating, sir?"

Lance winked. "Not in the way I thought, but I'm hoping you will help me take *stimulating* in a whole other direction."

****

Kate felt a tap on her shoulder. She angled her body and saw one of the only two faces in the room she recognized. "Hey, Jack."

"Please come with me, Ms. Taylor."

Jack's expression was somber and serious, matching the tone of his voice. Wondering what was wrong, Kate rose slowly.

"You can bring your things," he said.

A flash of panic raced through her. Everyone would surely notice if she was escorted out by the Senator's security team. If curiosity got the best of some attendees, her cover would be blown and so would be her chance to get out of the tabloid business. "I didn't mean anything by the geek comment." Her voice sounded raspy, and her hand actually shook as she gathered her purse and pushed her chair into place.

Jack stepped back. "This request has nothing to do with your conversation with the senator, ma'am."

"Miss," she reminded with a nervous smile.

"Yes, ma'am," Jack replied.

She saw another man with a telltale wire twisting over his ear take a position alongside the double doors leading to the kitchen. "I promise I am no threat to National Security." Jack's gaze stayed neutral.

"Follow me, please."

"Where are we going?"

He gestured to the swinging kitchen door. "Right through there, Ms. Taylor."

She pictured herself led away in handcuffs with a raincoat over her head. "Before I get dinner?"

"Looks that way."

As she walked alongside him, her mind whirled. "Am I on the no-fly list?"

"Don't know, ma'am," Jack replied.

"I'm not a terrorist."

Jack said nothing.

Had her real identity been discovered? "Am I being asked to leave the reunion for a specific reason?" Was it her imagination, or did she see Jack smile?

"You could say that, ma'am."

They almost reached the kitchen door when the left

door whooshed open, and four servers appeared each holding dinner plates.

Jack stepped to the right.

She pressed herself against the wall until they passed. "I really do love America," she whispered. She felt a wash of panic and gave one last look toward the dining room. No one appeared to have noticed her leaving. "If I'm not a threat to national security, tell me why I'm heading to the kitchen and missing dinner?"

Jack held open the right door. Kitchen sounds of dishes clanking, utensils dropping into sinks, and the sous-chef barking orders nearly drowned out his answer. "The senator asked to see you."

The tension in Kate's body suddenly released. She bit back a smile. "Well, all right then. Lead the way."

Chapter Four

Jack led the way through the kitchen to a room at the back.

She could hear snippets of conversations as she followed, but the kitchen noises were louder than the voices. The aroma of bread baking and sauces being stirred made her stomach rumble. She wished she'd eaten more than a handful of cheese curls for lunch.

Jack placed a palm on the rear door and held it open. "The senator has someone with him but is waiting inside."

"Maybe I shouldn't intrude."

"You won't be, ma'am."

"Miss," Kate said quickly. This time she did see him smile.

"The senator always has someone wanting to speak to him. I assure you the interruption is welcome."

Kate nodded. Out of the corner of her eye, she saw Jack take a sentry position to the right. She inhaled deeply and stepped inside a small office furnished with a few black cabinets, a metal desk, and two chairs, one of which was occupied by Senator Michaels listening to a man seated in the other.

As soon as Lance saw her, he rose. "Kate, you remember Paul Neely from class."

Paul turned.

The blank look on Paul's face told Kate he had no

idea who she was. "Why, yes." She extended a hand. "Voted most likely to...." She paused then laughed, "I wasn't at Ridgemont High long. Refresh my memory if I'm wrong. Most likely to succeed in business?"

"Sure was." Smiling, Paul stood and offered Kate the chair.

With a firm shake of her head, she declined.

Paul did not retake his seat.

"The prediction came true," Lance added. "Paul is CEO for a major pharmaceutical company in the area."

Kate quickly ran through a list of pharmas close by. "Questmeds?" She hoped she picked the right one.

"Yes." Paul confirmed. "I'm surprised you would know considering your short stay at Ridgemont."

Think, Kate! She saw an article in the local paper a few months ago about a drug coming off patent and the effect any generics produced by rival companies would have on the parent company. Hopefully that company was Quest, and the CEO was quoted in the copy. "I read an article about Zenathane."

Paul nodded. "Will be a tough year going forward for the company."

Kate had to change the tenor of the conversation. She punched a fist in the air. "I'll just bet you can help." Her mind spun. "Anyone elected most likely to succeed has skills." Her stomach churned, and she looked at Lance. "Right, Senator?"

"I agree. Not only was Paul president of the Business Club, he was also a darn good quarterback. Almost took us to the state finals in his senior year."

Paul squared his shoulders. "You weren't half bad either, Senator."

"I wish I was at the game. I could have cheered for

you both," Kate said.

Lance's and Paul's smiles faded.

"I transferred in January of my senior year." She began layering her story. "Awkward time to come to a new school."

"Oh, that's why you don't look familiar," Paul angled his body away. "Some final game, wasn't it, Senator Michaels?"

"Sure was. You sparked the team right up until the end." Lance shook his head. "If I hadn't missed the tackle, maybe the championship trophy would be in the case outside the gym."

Paul snickered. "You and half the team between the runner and the end zone missed tackles."

"You're too kind, and call me Lance. Senator is much too formal a title between friends."

Paul's chest puffed. "Lance it is." He glanced at Kate. "I suppose I'll leave you two here to get reacquainted."

Lance held out his hand. "Appreciate it, Paul. My schedule is pretty tight, and I'd like to catch up a little with Kate."

"Sure thing." Paul walked to the door then turned. "Hey, could you use a hand with the campaign?"

Lance nodded. "Always. I have some tough competition this time around."

"I'd be honored," Paul replied.

"I'll have my campaign manager get in touch about setting up a local headquarters near you." Lance pulled a business card from his inside jacket pocket. "Here's his name and number. He's at the regional campaign office in Princeton. If you don't hear something in a few days, give him a call."

Paul scanned the card and left.

Suddenly, Kate could not decide if she was equally as honored or just plain angry. She had just witnessed the consummate politician smooze. If Lance Michaels thought the political fluff talk would work on her, he was dead wrong. She squared her shoulders and waited for the political doublespeak to begin.

Lance angled the chair away from the desk. "Thanks for agreeing to join me. Please, make yourself comfortable." He loosened his tie and peeled off his suit jacket. After neatly folding the coat, he laid it atop the closest file cabinet. He turned and drew down his brows.

Kate had not moved. She stood with arms folded across her chest.

"Was it something I said?"

For a second, she hesitated before the words spilled from her mouth. "Not yet, but I expect soon."

His dark eyes narrowed. "I think we've had a bit of a misunderstanding."

"For you." The heat of anger snaked through her. "I might not be very politically savvy, but I do watch the occasional news story. Let's clear the air, shall we? I don't want to be an intern and move into an apartment a few blocks from yours in Washington." Her finger stabbed the air with each word. "I don't want to be your assistant, your go-fer, or your side chick. I like my job here just fine, so no funny stuff. Get me?"

"I see," Lance said after a moment's hesitation. He gave her a somber nod.

Kate lifted her chin, and her lips twisted in a satisfied smirk. "Glad we understand each other."

Two creases appeared on Lance's brow. "May I

ask what you do for a living to make you so passionate?"

What did she do? She couldn't tell him she was a reporter. She blurted out the first thing coming to mind. "I sell johnny ads." The look on Lance's face told her he had no idea what she meant. Truthfully, she'd only seen one, herself. She put her hands on her hips. "In the restroom at a restaurant or other venues, you find advertising spots on the back of the cubicle door giving you something to read while you—wait. I sell the ads."

Lance burst out laughing.

Kate rolled her eyes. "The job might not be the most glamorous, but it pays the rent."

"I can see a lot of similarities in what we do," he said, still smiling. "Last session, a lot of my colleagues thought my agenda belonged in the toilet." He snickered. "And not for reading."

The half smile creeping up her lips warred with the embarrassment inside her.

He held up his hands. "Before this meeting goes any farther, let me assure you I don't want an intern, I can't afford another apartment on The Beltway, and I don't have time for a side chick. I don't even have a…" He tilted his head. "What do they call the opposite of side chick these days?"

"Girlfriend." Kate skipped her gaze over his face as she thought about what just happened. Heat washed across her cheeks, and she grinned. "I might have over-reacted."

His smile widened. "You definitely did."

So much for first impressions, Kate thought, and sighed. "Guess we're done here."

He shook his head. "I'll give you a pass. Since you

aren't interested in politics, you probably wouldn't know I need to be just as cautious as you were a minute ago."

She exhaled sharply. "Says the man on the top of the food chain and immersed in power politics for the last six years." She screwed up. If she hadn't been so distracted by her ruse and his devastatingly good looks, she would have realized he had to be careful in the public eye. But now was not the time for confession. At the moment, she wasn't a reporter who knew how the media worked. She was a woman who sold bathroom advertisements for a living. His expression looked liked he had just taken a big swallow of spoiled milk.

He rocked back on his heels. "The problem is the tabloids. Nasty publications with even nastier reporters who call themselves journalists. You probably can't imagine walking by a newsstand and seeing your life, or rather, something made up about your life, in two-inch headlines. But I see stories like that about me regularly. *The Daily Dish* ruined the reputation of a good friend because of a well-placed lie of a bogus scandal. Sure, the story was retracted two weeks later but the disclaimer was buried in the back of the paper between ads and the crossword."

If guilt was the ocean, then she was paddling around in a leaky lifeboat during a hurricane. She wanted this assignment but now suspected getting some dirt on this ultra-cautious senator could be harder than she thought. His guard was up, and she had woven one big yarn about her life.

The increase of heat across her cheeks felt like the touch of a blowtorch without a valve. "Maybe we should start over once I get my foot out of my mouth."

She held out her right hand. "Kate Taylor. Toilet ad saleswoman." She caught what looked like a glimmer of amusement in his eyes.

He took her hand. "Lance Michaels. United States Senator."

"Nice to meet you, Senator."

His expression shifted. "Let's skip the formalities. Call me Lance Michaels."

Nodding, she gently eased free her hand. "Should I leave now that I've made a total fool of myself?"

"How about instead we engage in a little friendly conversation without either of us expecting the worst?" He gestured again to the chair.

She sat and covered her midsection with her hand. "Could be a plan, but I hope you can hear over the roar of my stomach rumbling. I was about to get my rib eye when your security guard whisked me away."

"I think I can help out." He walked to the door and signaled the first person he saw. 'Two steaks." He glanced over his shoulder. "Rare, medium or, God forbid, well."

"Medium rare."

He held up two fingers. "Medium rare."

"Calling in a political favor or promising one?" Kate asked.

"Neither." Lance walked to the chair opposite her and sat.

A server wheeled in a dining cart and set two places on the desk before retrieving two covered dishes and placing them between the silverware. He filled glasses with ice and sparkling water then left.

Lance lifted both silver covers and set them aside. "I'm just as hungry as you are."

"Good, then let's eat." He put a hand across his tie and sat. "If you don't want the filet, I'll get you something else."

"This will be fine." She smiled. So, being a senator did have its perks for selecting dinner at least.

****

Lance sipped his water, and over the rim of the glass, he studied the woman who had turned a dreaded campaign stop into something thoroughly enjoyable. She was pretty, intelligent, a little cautious, a whole lot bold, and she wasn't afraid to be honest with someone to whom others would normally begin each sentence with a yes. He hadn't met someone like her in years and a part of him wished he hadn't. She was just the kind of woman who had the potential to ruin his political career if he let her get close and the media found out.

****

The back-and-forth conversation over dinner lasted almost a full hour. Somewhere between the laughter and the serious conversation, Kate started to question if she could go through with the assignment. The all-in determination to begin her fact-finding about Lance Michaels the politician when she arrived now didn't interest her as much as the personal facts she wanted to know about Lance Michaels the man.

Without removing her gaze from his face, she lifted her glass and took two full swallows of water. "I really am sorry I accused you of philandering."

"No." He patted his chest. "You accused me of *thinking* about philandering."

"One and the same."

"Doublespeak for a politician." He drew a celery stick through a puddle of dressing before taking a bite.

"The media can take one small word from a slip of the tongue and destroy everything a legislator hoped to do while serving in office. A lot of politicians are wary of reporters twisting facts so they talk about doing a lot of things but never accomplish anything much except the opportunity to gather fodder for another broken campaign promise."

She snickered. "But not you."

"Nope. I'm more direct."

"You seriously want me to believe you're different." He didn't smile, but amusement lit his eyes.

"I am."

She slid an elbow onto the desk and rested her chin in her palm before catching his gaze and narrowing her eyes. "Convince me."

"Okay." He dabbed at the corners of his mouth and then folded his napkin. "I could have had my Chief of Staff find you on the registration list and invite you to the next campaign event. Then he'd put you at my table so I could get to know you without using a wingman."

A puzzled frown puckered her eyebrows. "So instead of formalities, you chose to use drama to practically scare the life out of me. Your henchman almost had me convinced I was some sort of enemy of the state."

His mouth formed a slanting grin. "Jack isn't a henchman, but he would be interested why you would conclude something so sinister."

She fought a returning smile threatening to break free. "You're kidding, right? A tall, muscular guy with an earpiece and an expression like one of the presidents on Mount Rushmore says 'Miss, come with me and bring your things'." She put out her hands, wrists together. "All I could envision was a pair of handcuffs on my wrists and a raincoat over my head."

Lance's smile broke free. "I just wanted to meet you away from the crowd and the ensuing whispers if I spent a little too much time talking to you in the buffet line."

She snickered. "You actually think no one wondered where I was going with your security guy."

Lance shrugged. "I suppose some might be a tad curious."

"I know I'd want to find out."

They fell silent for a moment. Kate glanced at her empty plate. Dinner was over, but she wasn't ready to leave. When she looked up Lance had an elbow propped on the table, jaw to knuckle, staring.

Curious about his scrutiny, she hunted for a way to continue the evening for a while. "I do have a question. Why don't you have a significant other?" She saw his smile drop.

"Politicking takes a lot of time."

Kate crossed her arms and leaned back. "A weak excuse. I'm sure dozens of women would love a shot."

Lance's shoulders shot up in a nonchalant shrug. "I'm not interested in a Washington socialite. Politics attract a certain kind of women, and those particular women do not give up until they become a wife or at the very least, a girlfriend."

"You're profiling." Humor tinged her words.

"Maybe I am."

"From the newspaper stories lately about politicians and the women who love them, maybe you aren't."

Lance squared his shoulders. "I wouldn't call the

allegations in some of those stories love. While some might be true, some could also be publicity stunts or revenge for an ended affair or a spurned mistress."

"And you have nothing to worry about?" She narrowed her eyes. "Oh, that's right. You don't have a girlfriend." She saw his smile fade.

"Well, there is a girl...friend." He spaced a long pause between the last two words. "We see each other occasionally. She helps me not be conspicuously solo when I attend serious state dinners or other events I can't avoid. She understands the D.C. social concept of being single."

She had skipped over that part of articles she'd read about him. She raised her eyebrows. "Explain please."

"The power-brokering of social events."

Kate drew down her brows. "A concept needing clarification." His smile awakened a dimple. She almost smiled back.

"Explaining will take more time than I have right now," he replied.

Her eyes narrowed. "But you have enough time to resort to intrigue to meet me." She pressed her lips together and nodded. "Interesting."

Lance laughed. "You sound more like a reporter than an ad saleswoman."

The heat of awkwardness rose on Kate's chest, and she fought a blush by taking a long drink of cold water. "I should warn you, I'm a November baby, and the word is anyone born in the eleventh month can't control their mouths."

"No filter, huh?"

"None."

"Could be a problem."

She sighed. "Usually is."

"Hmm," he mumbled with a nod.

Kate tilted her head. "Hmm? Meaning?"

"Just how it sounded."

"Sounds to me like you don't know how to respond." Her mind had to backtrack to the last time she enjoyed any conversation as much as she did this one.

He snickered. "You caught me."

As she saw a ghost of laughter gleam in his eyes, Kate felt uncharacteristically relaxed. "Before this conversation hits a wall and you say something dismissing, I would like to know a little more about you."

"You stole my next line." He leaned back. "What would you like to know?"

She shrugged. "I'm told all politicians always have an agenda of some sort."

He winked. "Professionally or personally?"

"Politically," she said with emphasis. "I'd hate to think my initial," she stopped and winked back, "impression of you was correct." She eased her elbow onto the table, rested her chin on her fist, and stared him dead in his eyes. "So, what's your plan for the next six years, providing you win the election?"

Lance tilted his head and paused for a moment. "You make an agenda sound sinister."

"They can be."

He rested his forearms on the table and leaned forward, his gaze never wavering. "I don't scheme."

Kate blinked. "Okay, I'll concede the point for the moment. What's your strategy to save democracy?"

"I'd like to get closer to a balanced federal budget and still give the military the money needed to make America safe, but then something else would have to go."

"Such as?"

He shrugged. "I might need a few more terms to figure out the specifics."

Kate threw back her head and laughed. "What else?"

"I'd love to somehow get the pharmaceutical drug companies to make life-saving drugs more affordable, especially for our seniors. That's why I spoke to Paul. I especially want to tackle funding for orphan diseases and the opioid crisis in the country." He closed his eyes and shook his head. His eyes opened then captured her gaze again. "Such a waste of lives."

His determined voice and sober gaze confirmed he was serious and not just repeating electioneering points. He might actually be one of the good guys, but she couldn't let anything change her focus. "Which of the two would you tackle first?"

"Both. Just because some diseases are rare, those afflicted matter as much as any other person." He looked away for a moment. "As far as the opioid epidemic, too many lives are being destroyed. We have to somehow find a way to help them."

"Sounds personal," she said in a gentle voice. She saw him swallow hard.

"It is. I lost a cousin to addiction. My aunt's only son. Worst of all, no one knew he was not only using but also selling to support his habit until he was arrested." His eyes darkened. "The whole tragedy nearly destroyed the family."

The pain in his voice was real. Kate reached out and touched his hand. "I'm so sorry. I should not have asked."

Squaring his shoulders, he took a deep breath. "Asking is the only way to get something done. My cousin's situation is one of the reasons I'm running for re-election. I've sponsored a few bills in the Senate, and if I'm not re-elected, they probably won't find a sponsor and be re-posted in the next session."

Kate patted the back of his hand. "Then let's hope you are successful."

Lance tilted his head. "You're taking a side in the election? What happened to the I-hate-politics girl?"

She grinned. "Let's just say I'm open to worthy causes."

"It's a start."

With a half glance in his direction, she wondered what an election campaign for someone who cared more about causes than the celebrity associated with an office on Capitol Hill might be like. Deciding against going down that road, she raised an eyebrow and shot him a warning gaze. "Not so fast. I just got here, and the jury is still out."

"Fair enough."

The conversation continued for another hour until a knock preceded the door opening.

Jack leaned inside, one hand on the doorknob, the other on the frame. "Sir, I think the attendees are getting restless. Several have asked about you."

He raised a hand. "I'll be right there."

Nodding, Jack shut the door.

Lance stood and circled the desk. "My cue to get back to business."

Acknowledging the pleasant meeting was over, Kate rose.

"Thanks for joining me." He put out a hand.

Since she always was more laid back than formal, without thinking and at the same time, Kate raised her arms to hug him.

Lance chuckled, lowered his hand, and leaned forward to accept the embrace.

But Kate had already switched gestures, her hand now extended between them.

As if on cue, each looked at the other and laughed.

The evening had not been a very professional way of conducting a covert fact-gathering meeting, but she didn't care. Something about Lance Michaels had gotten to her. Spending time with him blurred the hard edges she'd come to expect from D.C. politicians. Though she hadn't had time to examine all his good points, apparently her hormones had. If she thought she would be meeting a normally self-serving politician, she was dead wrong. Lance Michaels did not fit the mold in the least. "I guess I should go out and join my fellow alumni."

"And I'll do one more circle of the room and be on my way." He opened his arms. "But before I go, I would like the hug we let pass a few seconds ago."

Kate answered with a dimpled grin and stepped into the circle his arms made. He barely touched her but when she looked in his eyes, she could feel the muscles in his shoulders tense.

"Kate, I—"

His voice held a definite tightness. She glanced at the curve of his lips then looked into his eyes and waited. "Oh heck," she muttered. "What happens next can't be good."

"No, it can't," he replied.

His fingers tangled in her hair as he drew her head close. His lips caressed then took hers again and again until her breath came in quick shallow gulps. First came tender, tentative kisses then hard, hungry kisses, making her heart pound. His hand never left the back of her head and her fingers never moved from his cheeks. When he lifted his head and released her, she felt suddenly denied.

His gaze lingered on her lips before he traced her mouth with a thumb. "I think I am out of order."

"I didn't hear the sound of a gavel pounding, and you might have noticed I didn't complain." Warmth spread across her cheeks.

His mouth tightened. "Still, I was out of line."

Not wanting him to have any regrets for something that felt so right, she wondered for a minute how to end the night. A handshake would be too formal given the situation and a kiss not wise. She put a hand on his shoulder. "Maybe, maybe not."

He released her and rocked back on his heels. He gave her a very masculine head nod. "I'm glad you came."

She dipped her head. "I'm glad I came, too."

He smiled and walked away.

As he did she called out, "Lance."

Turning, he stared.

The puzzled look on his face spoke volumes. "I'm glad I had dinner with you." His smile lit the dim room.

"I am, too." His gaze held hers for a moment before he headed out the door and into the reunion.

Shaken by the jumble of unanticipated thoughts

racing through her brain, Kate stared after him. The lingering echo of pleasure both surprised and intoxicated. Her heart still pounded. She touched her kiss-swollen lips. Kissing Lance wasn't how she pictured the high school reunion would end. What in the heck happened?

****

Jack pulled onto the highway and headed toward Princeton. He glanced at his boss in the rearview mirror. "You haven't stopped smiling since we left the reunion."

Lance had been staring out the side window, Kate on his mind since he left the venue. Turning, he caught Jack's gaze in the mirror. "Sure haven't."

The answer made both Jack and the security officer in the passenger seat grin. "You had a good time then, sir?"

"I had a very interesting time."

"Wasn't very *stimulating* though?" Jack's grin widened.

"Didn't need to be. Not tonight, Jack. Being at the reunion was more enjoyable for a campaign stop than I thought possible."

Again, Jack glanced into the rearview mirror. "Kate?"

Lance nodded. "She's not like the women I normally meet. She's grounded and sure of herself." He laughed. "I like those traits. I mean what woman would actually admit she sells restroom ads for a living within five minutes of meeting someone?"

"Restroom ads?"

"Supposedly on the back of the stall doors, though I've never actually seen one. Have you?"

"I can't say I've lingered long enough to notice," Jack said over the chuckle of his partner.

Lance fell silent for a moment. "I want to see her again."

"You'll have plenty of time after the election, sir."

He thought about the grassroots campaign stops already scheduled, the endless hours he'd be spending on the campaign trail, and the time commuting between New Jersey and Washington to do the job for which he was elected and rejected Jack's suggestion. "I don't want to wait until then."

"Do you think you can politic and develop a relationship at the same time?"

"I'll make it work." Lance could see seriousness in Jack's eyes reflected in the rearview mirror. "Though I can only see you from the middle of your nose up, I can tell you don't agree."

Jack made a right turn at the end of the ramp and headed the truck toward Lance's home in Mercer County. "We don't know much about her, sir, and you have some serious competition for your senate seat this time around. You know the media. Reporters climb over each other for a chance to dig around and find something to twist into shock value, whether the concept is fact or fiction." He brought the truck to a stop at a red light and angled his body so he could look directly at Lance. "I could run a quick background check to put your mind at ease."

"You mean to put *your* mind at ease." He would not resort to undercover work to decide if he should continue a relationship. He'd rather rely on faith. Lance shook his head. "Let's hold off for the moment. Right now, I prefer to think principles top deception."

"Not in D.C.," Jack replied.

"But we're not in D.C., so let me enjoy this little breath of fresh air for now." Lance pointed forward. "Green light."

Jack rotated and started driving.

In silence, Lance watched the landscape speed by. Maybe Jack had a point. A background check on Kate would be sensible. Almost at the same time the thought entered his mind, he chided himself for being such a cynic and pushed away the notion. Kate wasn't like anyone he'd met since he became a senator. He would rely on his instincts and not dig into Kate's personal life, especially since the reward for his gut feeling could be a possible relationship.

****

Kate was barely home five minutes when her cell phone signaled a text message. She glanced at the screen. Gartman. Debating whether to read the text, she hovered an index finger over the display. Though she'd rather ignore him, she read his message.

—*What have you got for me?*—

—*Nothing.*—

—*I didn't send you there to eat rubber chicken and cake. I want copy to my inbox by noon.*—

Kate stared at the text for about five minutes. She had no choice. She hadn't won the lottery and needed this job. As she reached to turn off the light, she suspected her thoughts would once again keep her from a restful slumber. Only this time those thoughts would not be about looking for a better place to work. They would be about choosing between fulfilling her job and furthering her budding relationship with the man whose reputation she could ruin with an internet posting.

Chapter Five

A few days later, Kate stood on the sidewalk outside the auditorium at Lexington Community College. Along with a few hundred others, she attended the first of what she suspected would be many town hall meetings hosted by a local political group. The agenda for the event noted the program consisted of a short speech followed by some questions and answers.

She glanced at the velvet-covered roping hanging from portable metal posts lining the walkway all the way to the door. So, this setup is a rope line. She never waited in one and never had the desire to do so. No rock star, sports hero or politician could be important enough for her to wait for hours for a glimpse. She squeezed between a teenage boy with a buzz cut wearing a patriotic T-shirt and a middle-aged couple deep in discussion with a small group of college students and settled in a spot behind them. From the snippets of conversation, the students and the couple debated the pros and cons of one of the senator's position papers.

She sighed. So far the experience was not very exciting, and she was already a few hours into the assignment, including time she spent brushing up on Lance's politics the night before. He expressed some interesting opinions and ideas, but the concepts seemed innovative and would be tough to get accepted in the current uncommunicative atmosphere on Capitol Hill. Although after reading a few of his speeches and the statements of the bills he sponsored or signed on to, she could understand why he wanted another six-year term.

More supporters arrived, many dressed in red, white, and blue and clutching small, handmade signs containing words of support. Most wore the campaign buttons from his first run at the senate seat. The man and woman standing beside her wore a lot more than one. She counted about ten buttons with various slogans...obviously big supporters.

The woman met Kate's gaze. "First-timer?"

Kate nodded.

"You couldn't have picked a better place to start. Senator Michaels is one of the good ones."

"You know him?"

The bespectacled woman shook her head. "Not personally, but his stand on most issues mirrors my own."

The pulse of the people. Maybe I can get a lead here. "Which matter in particular?" Any answer forthcoming was swallowed by the rolling roar of applause that began with supporters standing in parking lot A and rippled toward her like water broken by a tossed rock.

"He's here," the woman shouted. She pressed forward into the velvet rope. She pointed. "Here he comes."

Kate watched Jack exit a large black car and scan the area like radar finding a target. He walked to the passenger door, hesitated, and then pulled it open.

Lance emerged and acknowledged the cheering with a wave. His easy gait as he walked from his car to the rope line contrasted sharply with the movements of his flanking security team.

As he moved up the line shaking hands he saw her, and his smile evolved from a small bow to an ear-to-ear curl. "Ms. Taylor. I'm surprised to see you here." He reached for her hand.

She slipped her hand into his. When she did, a ripple of pleasure shot through her. She couldn't determine if the feeling was from his touch or his acknowledgment of her and couldn't waste time deciding which. Like it or not, she had a job to do. "I'm surprised myself." His firm-but-gentle hold did not release.

"Last time we met, you made it perfectly clear just how much you dislike politics."

Her gaze held his. "Just maybe you are really a silver-tongued statesman and convinced me to get involved."

Lance laughed. "I sincerely doubt it, but I will take the compliment."

"Senator Michaels. Over here." The woman standing next to Kate pushed her way toward him.

Lance broke contact with Kate.

The woman extended a hand. "If I can help you, please let me know. I'll stuff envelopes, make calls, do anything at any time. My husband and I are ready to do whatever it takes to get you another term."

The man with her chuckled. "I'm right here, Norma, and I can speak for myself." He shook Lance's hand. "She's a gusher, Senator. "Talks about your record to anyone who'll listen."

Lance nodded to Norma. "I appreciate your support. I can sure use help at my campaign office." He gestured to a young man behind. "Please give my aide, Sam, your contact information. Someone from the campaign will call you in the morning."

Norma beamed. "Thank you."

Sam gestured for Norma to follow him, and they walked away from the crowd.

Lance put his hand on Kate's arm. "How about getting some coffee after the speech?"

Kate angled her head. "Are you asking me out, Senator?"

He looked at the ground and laughed before looking back. "Politicians don't date during campaign season, Ms. Taylor. I'd just like to continue our discussion on a strictly friendly level, of course."

She was flattered his smile told her otherwise. "And I would like you to explain the position paper you wrote on offshore drilling. I find it rather contradictory in some areas." As the initial cheering turned into more of a grumbling, she lifted her chin. She looked right and saw some supporters craning their necks down the line in her direction. "But for now, the proverbial natives are getting restless, and your adoring public waits."

Lance nodded and slowly moved on.

With a mixture of admiration and awe, she watched him greet the people. His body language and expression engaged each as though he knew him or her personally. If charisma translated into votes, she suspected Lance would win in a landslide. She felt, rather than saw, someone approach.

"Ms. Taylor."

She recognized the voice and glanced over her shoulder. "Jack. Nice to see you."

With a swipe of his hand, he gestured to his left.

"Please come with me."

"Again?" She grinned.

Jack just smiled.

She walked with him toward a side entrance. "You know, Jack, you really need to find a better pick-up line."

He laughed. "Does the senator need one?"

Kate started to answer but pressed her lips into a tight grin instead. Until she figured out how she felt about Lance she didn't want to confirm or deny anything. The two together just didn't make any sense. She normally prided herself on being sensible and responsible, but around Lance, she felt anything but rational. She sensed Jack knew her story contained a lot more. Telling him anything would reveal too much information, because no matter how much she convinced herself she was only doing her job, she wondered what being foolish for a change might be like.

****

For about forty-five minutes backstage and off to the right, Kate watched Lance take questions from the audience.

The man stood. "Dennis Smith, the *Daily Informer*. I'd like your take on an article appearing on web this morning, Senator."

She could see Lance's brow furrow, but he smiled nonetheless. He almost made it through the event without a question about her story. Thinking about how he would respond, she felt her stomach clench.

"A lot of things go up on the web, Mr. Smith. Could you be a bit more specific?"

Smith turned the tablet he held toward the stage.

"I'm referring to the story in today's *Analytical*. The headline reads: *Thirty-eight and no date. Is Senator Michaels hiding a secret life?* The gist of the piece questions your sexual preference."

For a moment, Lance stared out at the audience and offered a smile that quickly faded. "I haven't read the piece, so commenting before I do would be pointless."

"Are you hiding something, Senator?" Smith paged through the small notebook he held then looked up. "I'd like a quote."

Kate saw Lance visibly bristle.

A frown briefly formed on his lips before he controlled his expression. "Because I didn't bring a date to a town meeting?"

His tone sounded sharp. He was getting angry. Angry interview subjects did not think clearly and usually said things they regretted. She never believed in telepathy, but maybe now was the time to try out some. She fixed her gaze on Lance. *Easy now. Don't let that guy bait you.*

"Because you aren't seen with women very often." The reporter scrolled down his tablet. "I can't find one piece over the last year showing you with the same woman more than twice." He looked up. "Care to comment?"

"No, I don't," Lance answered. "My personal life has nothing to do with my politics."

If she got through to Lance via ESP, she'd never know because the reporter continued to reference her story to make his point. Her heartbeat rose. She'd written a quick article on Lance's solitary road life because she had copy to turn in. The words she penned were benign or so she thought. She found Lance to be the gentleman everyone said he was and had a hard time eking out the few words she did send off to Gartman. She had not written about a possible secret life. When the article appeared online, she should have checked for edits. If she knew Gartman edited the heck out of her copy, she would have made him take down the story. With the reporter from the *Informer* using the narrative to back Lance into a corner, all bets were off.

The heat of anger grew on her cheeks. Gartman had no right to turn her piece into an inquisition on Lance's home life. She pulled out her phone to reread the article then changed her mind. Okay, maybe he did. She didn't want to over-think what he might have done to the story. *The Analytical* was a tabloid, and he was the editor-in-chief. She would definably be more careful with the next round of copy she turned in.

Because of the white noise of embarrassment ringing in her ears, she missed much of the back and forth between Lance and Smith. When she finally focused, the discussion was over.

The moderator stood. "I want to thank you all for coming. Now let's allow the senator to get back out on the campaign trail and then on to another term in Washington."

The applause was long and loud when Lance stood and acknowledged obvious approval from the crowd before leaving the stage.

Kate hoped Smith's question would fade to black and disappear but feared the opposite. She knew tabloid reporters; she was one. Their job was to pick apart people's lives like vultures feeding on an animal carcass and then run like Hades to print with a feature about an errant fact or a farfetched theory. Even though she had to pen another juicy tidbit soon, the guilt building in her gut had her spinning ways to make Gartman print a retraction for this one.

Amidst fading applause, Lance stepped into the backstage shadows and saw Jack among the faces in the small crowd waiting to escort him out. He frowned and shook his head.

"Brutal, sir," Jack replied.

"First time something like my dating habits ever came up." Lance pressed together his lips before speaking again. "I can't imagine why."

Guilt welled inside Kate. She stepped around Jack. "Maybe the question was just a case of an overzealous cub reporter making a name for herself." She held her breath and hoped no one picked up on her pronoun use.

"Kate. I'm glad you're here."

The light was back in his eyes. His forced smile underlined how he felt. She fought back the unease growing in her gut. "Maybe now isn't the best time."

A dip of his head and a slight shrug answered her. "In my line of work, a good time never exists."

Jack stepped forward. "Should I ask the fact-checker to get on this story?"

"No." Lance shot back. "I don't want to give credence to the article and watch the innuendo grow legs and run." He blew out a short breath. "The fact-checker already has plenty of work. I'm sure a lot more conjecture and opinion pieces will come out over the next few weeks."

"You aren't worried about your reputation?" Kate drew down her brows. "I mean, won't the story cost you some votes?"

Lance chuckled. "You are definitely an election

rookie. Voters change their minds all the time. That's why polls have a margin of error built into the statistics and are sometimes wrong all together. I'm used to opponents tossing out half-truths and edited sound bites. Trash stories don't keep me up at night much." He pointed toward her forehead. "And if you keep frowning, you will etch some serious wrinkles there."

Kate raised her eyebrows in an exaggerated stretch and rubbed her forehead with her fingertips. "I can always get some filler."

A hint of a smile brightened his features, and his eyes glittered. "You're perfect just the way you are."

Kate forced a smile to mask the guilt. If only he knew just how imperfect she was.

Jack gestured toward the exit, and the entourage moved forward.

"How much did you hear?" Lance asked.

"Not a whole lot." She narrowed her eyes. "Are you worried?"

Jack scanned the area. "I could get Maxie to help out. She'd come to the next few campaign stops, stand next to you, and smile."

Kate stopped walking. A twinge of curiosity swept up her spine. "Who's Maxie?"

Lance turned. "A friend."

"With benefits?" Kate asked. She wished she could smile to make the comment sound like a joke, but she was serious. She wanted to know.

Lance shook his head. "Only if you think hanging around stuffy career politicians and lobbyists for hours on a Saturday night is a benefit."

Kate broke eye contact and cleared her throat. "Guess not."

Jack pulled out his cell phone and searched the contact list. "Maxie wouldn't mind helping out."

"I would." Lance lifted his chin. "Hang up."

Jack cocked his head while raising his eyebrows and disconnected the call.

"Maxie's sudden appearance will only invite more conjecture. Besides, I'd be asking her to pretend to be in a relationship that doesn't exist." Lance sucked in a deep breath and then expelled the words like a rapid-fire semiautomatic. "I won't do that. I can't."

A little jumping smile tugged one side of Kate's mouth. Lance didn't want to play games. He was one of the good ones.

The rear exit door of the auditorium opened. Another member of the security team stepped inside and shut the door behind him. "We are ready for you, sir."

"Straight shot to the RV?" Lance asked.

Jack shook his head. "Probably not. A small crowd is outside."

"Stay close." Lance took Kate's hand. "We're going out."

Kate hesitated. Someone might recognize her. "You want me to come along?"

"I do. I'm heading to Princeton to my campaign office. If you ride along, we can get to know each other a little better without having to worry about who might be watching."

"What about my car? I drove here."

"Give your keys to Jack, and let him know where the car is parked. He'll get it to the campaign office. We'll meet him there."

His gaze caught hers, and she felt as though she fell

into his eyes. Her breath hitched as she wavered.

"You can leave whenever you want," he said.

She eased her hand free, dug the car keys out of her purse, and tossed them to Jack. "Black SUV in the first row. Probably with a couple of tickets under the wiper blades." She winked. "No parking zone. The lot was full, and I was late." She pivoted toward Lance. "Don't worry. I won't ask you to fix any summons I might have gotten."

Lance grinned. "Not something I would anyway."

Kate put her free hand on her chest and feigned surprise. "What do we have here? A rare honest politician?" She pulled out a cell phone and snapped his picture. "Like the elusive unicorn, I need something to prove I actually saw one."

The members of Lance's security team laughed.

"Believe me, you saw one." Jack winked. "Maybe the only one."

For a second Lance looked at the ground. "A lot of other politicians are serious about their work."

Jack raised an eyebrow and leaned back, but the veneer faded when Lance's expression steeled.

A sour tang rose from her stomach. *Am I out to ruin a good man?* Her smile fell.

"Something wrong?" Lance asked.

With a barely perceptible shake of her head, Kate sent her doubts to the recesses of her mind. She had a job, and she would do it. "No, just thinking."

"About me?"

"Not this soon. I barely know you." She saw disappointment bloom in his eyes.

"Let me add some details on the way to Princeton." Lance put his hand on the small of her back and gestured toward the door.

She nodded and got in step beside him as his team formed a protective triangle around them.

At the exit, the support team stopped. "We want to do one more quick check. Wait here please," a team member cautioned. He opened the door and disappeared outside.

"Are campaign stops always this crazy?" Kate asked.

"Afraid so," Lance replied. "The world is topsy-turvy these days, and people are very passionate about what they believe. Sometimes, a few go too far right or too far left and do things they regret. For now, personally paid security is the only answer to keeping the crazies at bay."

Ever the steadfast watcher, Jack stood between them and the back door of the venue—one hand on the exit bar, the other near his waist.

Kate leaned toward Lance. "Jack is carrying?" Her whispered voice wavered.

Lance put his hands on her upper arms and turned her toward him. "I don't want you to worry. The crowd out there is my base. All supporters. Nothing will happen."

Kate scanned his face and then glanced at Jack. "You didn't answer the question," she whispered.

"Exactly." He dipped his head. "Ready?"

She nodded and her mind moved to the worst case scenario—someone calling out her real name. Her first reaction was to run as images of what-could-be flashed through her mind, but she held her ground.

"If we get separated, a member of my team will get you to the RV."

Though a nagging ache of tension settled between her shoulder blades, she kept her gaze steady on his face. She saw his wink and another wave of guilty conscience rose. *What am I doing here? I could ruin this man.* She had no time to think, because Jack had already pushed open the door.

When the crowd noticed, a sound came like a buzzing of swarming bees. Those waiting surged forward almost as one solid object when Lance emerged from inside the building. With security on either side and Jack scanning the throng in front, he walked to the first person in line.

Kate watched him inch down the row, grasp outstretched hands, pose for selfies, and speak to each person who called his name. One moment he was visible, the next he disappeared inside a circle of citizens.

Jack touched her shoulder. "Waiting for the senator to finish speaking with his supporters could take a while." He gestured to a young man standing near the RV.

Kate watched the young man jog toward them.

"This is Sam." Jack looked toward the crowd. "I hope you don't mind if I get back to the line?"

By the way his body language shouted, Kate knew he was antsy. "Not at all," she replied.

Sam swept a hand through the air. "Follow me, please."

Kate nodded and walked in silence beside him.

"Make yourself comfortable inside," Sam said when they reached the RV. He looked back at the crowd.

Kate followed his gaze. "Go on. Jack might need

you."

"Thank you, ma'am." Sam jogged toward the crowd.

Kate put her hand on the grab bar mounted next to the door and climbed two steps. She turned and saw Lance talking to a boy holding one of Lance's campaign posters. Even at this distance, she could see the intensity on Lance's face. She watched Lance take the boy's cell phone and snap a selfie with him. He handed back the phone and waited until the young supporter boy checked the shot before speaking to a man and woman Kate guessed were the boy's parents.

About the time the conversation with the couple ended, Lance's security team spread their arms and ushered the remaining crowd toward their cars.

Lance turned his head and gestured for them to stop. He walked to the small group and started shaking hands.

Kate's knee-jerk smile did nothing to diminish a rising pang of guilt. Senator Lance Michaels really *was* a nice guy. She felt more uncertainty than ever about her assignment. With a downward glance, she entered the RV.

The inside was amazing with tons of high-end features. A wide-open living area looked comfortable with an L-shaped sofa and flat-screen television mounted on the wall. A leather, bench-seat dinette bordering a spacious kitchen with stainless steel appliances, quartz countertops, glossy wood cabinets, designer tile on the floor, and LED lighting in the ceiling. As she walked through the space, she skimmed a palm across the rich wood surfaces. The motor home felt bigger than her townhouse, and she wondered why anyone would need something so large just for campaigning. Maybe the time on the road was more taxing than she imagined.

She slipped into the bench seat at the dinette and shoved open the curtains covering a large window. The crowd had thinned. After speaking to the lingering supporters, Lance waved and jogged away.

As if on cue, the driver started the engine. A slight vibration rumbled under her feet, and for a moment when Lance entered and walked toward her, she couldn't differentiate between the RV shaking and her body trembling.

She caught his direct gaze. Lord, he had the most remarkable eyes. When he reached her, she saw his smile widen and a ripple of interest move across his face. "Nice ride," she said. "Taxpayer money?" She saw his smile instantly drop.

"No, mine. I have it rented until the end of the campaign."

"Then what?"

"Back to the RV lot for six years if I win." He slid into the bench seat opposite her. "Sam is on his way to my campaign office with your car. But if you would rather, I can radio him your address and drive you straight home."

She wasn't sure she wanted Lance to know where she lived. She shook her head. "I'd rather drive myself home." Her tone sounded clipped, and she hoped her smile would let him know she was being sensible.

Frowning, he drew back. "I wasn't suggesting anything sinister."

She heard the clear apology in his tone and moved back.

"Unless we agree right now my intentions are purely honorable, this thirty-minute ride to Princeton will seem awfully long and awfully cold."

Kate thought for a moment. He was right. So far he was the perfect gentleman, and she had no reason to think he would flip on the player switch now. "Agreed."

Smiling, he leaned forward and angled his body toward the front. "We're ready back here."

"Okay, sir," the driver acknowledged.

The RV moved, and Kate experienced an overwhelming sense of indecision wash over her. Was she doing the right thing? They would be alone for the next thirty minutes. Would she let her true identity slip out? Would the conversation cause Lance to somehow see through her guise? When she was with him, she could barely concentrate. Would they circle each other waiting for one to make the first move, or would they go full speed ahead and possibly do things neither should? True, a slip in the conversation could produce the golden fact she needed for her story, but it could also be the total undoing of her career. She closed her eyes and took a calming breath. No turning back now.

As the motor home pulled away from the venue, Lance pressed a button mounted behind him. A privacy screen descended from the ceiling and separated the driver's compartment from the rest of the motor home.

Kate furrowed her brow. "Honorable intentions?" She pointed to the partition. "Then what's that? I doubt that comes standard."

Lance laughed. "It doesn't, and I apologize for not warning you. I tweak my campaign speeches between stops to tailor the content to local issues. My driver, Ed, loves to debate on everything from what brand of coffee I drink to trade agreements with China. I had the divider added last campaign season so I could get some work done. I could open it if you would feel more comfortable, but then our conversation would definitely be a three-way."

She looked from the screen to his face. "When you put it that way, I'm good." But inside, she wasn't sure how she felt. Streetlights flashed past the large window as the motor home picked up speed. For the first time in a long time, Kate did not feel in control. *This situation is so not good. I should just tell him I need to leave as soon as we get to Princeton. I do have copy to turn in.* But when she spoke again, nothing close to her thoughts came out. "I can't stay long. I have an early sales call in the morning."

"You can leave whenever you'd like. Except when the RV is moving."

His lips lifted in a smile that made her breath catch. She closed her eyes to shut out the vision. "Obviously." She opened her eyes. "That's weird."

Lance tilted his head, and his forehead furrowed. "Are you getting carsick? I can have Ed pull over."

"No need." She almost laughed out loud but stifled the urge. "I kind of feel like I'm on a first date." Kate saw Lance's eyes ignite with two distinct reactions. The first relaxed his expression with what she thought might be relief. The second was definitely humor, and his cheeks dimpled.

"I was afraid you were having second thoughts."

She gave him a half smile. "Not yet."

The cat-and-mouse game they played brought on a sudden rush of conscience. She tempered the feeling by reminding herself good reporters got facts any way possible. Alone in a moving vehicle with the subject of an assignment was as good a way as any. But her heart reacted to Lance like no tabloid reporter's should. His smile curled her toes, stoking rising warmth she frankly did not want to extinguish. If she would ever do her job, she could not allow him to slip in and out of her thoughts the way he had all evening. She forced herself into reporter mode. "You spent a lot of time with that young boy. Is he a fan of yours?"

Lance settled back in the bench seat. "Actually, I'm a fan of his. His name is Joey Heywood. He was born with an ultra-rare bone condition. Only eight people in New Jersey have the disease and only a few hundred in the world."

Curious, Kate straightened. "What disease is so atypical?"

"They call it the Tin Man's disease. It is a debilitating genetic condition affecting bone growth."

Concern laced Lance's tone, and she saw mist in his eyes. "What happens?" Her voice was no more than a whisper.

His lips pressed together in a grimace. "Movement gets extremely limited. In some cases, no mobility remains." He looked away and then back. "Unless a cure is found, Joey has to be very careful and adjust everyday activities in order to have as normal a life as possible. His bones are very fragile."

Seeing the lines on Lance's brow deepen, Kate realized his involvement with this illness was not a political proclamation, but a cause for which he would fight. A despairing sigh escaped her lips, but she held her emotions in control. "How did you meet Joey?"

For a moment he hesitated. "When I settled into my D.C. office, Joey and his parents came in to ask if I would consider continuing the work of the senator I replaced. The disease is so rare not much money is in the federal budget to research a cause and a cure." He leaned forward and flattened his palms against the table." Most of the funding goes for ailments affecting a much wider part of the world's population. I call rare syndromes like Joey's stepchild afflictions. Disorders like his are not as far-reaching but are just as deadly and debilitating to families as the more recognized illnesses getting funding. Once I met Joey, I was hooked."

His sad smile looked genuine, and her determination to think solely about work was rattled by the depth of conviction she heard in his voice. The means to help families dealing with the terrible disease through federal funding branded itself upon his heart, and her job was to rip that spirit from his chest. Her next paycheck might just consist of thirty pieces of silver. Emotion clogged her throat, but she swallowed the remorse. "Do you know where the funding stands in the current budget?"

He tipped his head to the side. "Not entirely. Why do you ask?"

He sounded surprised she asked the question. Was she putting up red flags by delving into areas a toilet sales rep wouldn't know to ask? "I didn't think I'd get into fiscal dollars and cents, but seeing you with Joey has brought up so many questions, most of them starting with why."

"It's okay. Ask me anything."

"In a cajillion dollar federal budget, why is setting

aside money for ailments like his so hard? Why doesn't the government help?"

"Methodology."

She caught a flare of irritation in his eyes. "In government? How so?"

"I'm embarrassed to admit it, but getting a budget appropriation all boils down to the return-on-the-dollar principle. The budget office won't include a line item projecting inadequate categorical results to justify the appropriation. Millions of taxpayers can relate to research for cancer, but only a couple hundred families around the world will benefit from genetic study on Joey's disorder."

Kate cocked her head. "You are kidding."

He started to speak but then abruptly stopped, looked away, and shook his head.

When he faced her again, his features had softened, but pain filled his gaze. He really cared. Heaviness settled in her chest. She would ruin him and maybe his cause along with it. She suddenly did not like herself very much.

"I wish I were." He stared for a very long minute. "Until I can find a way to convince my colleagues funding for orphan diseases is worth a line item in the federal budget, I do what I can."

His words sounded deep and powerful, as though they'd come from someone other than a politician, but rather like someone affected personally. Kate slid her elbow onto the table and set her chin on top of her knuckles. "Interesting."

"How so?" He rested his clasped hands on the table.

Her eyebrows lifted a notch. "I didn't think a high-profile politician who offered his name and time to a worthy cause without a whole shoot-load of promised votes really existed, but I find myself sitting across from one."

A dull ache of regret rose in her belly. Was this guy for real? Was he as genuine as he appeared, or was he merely handing her a line he thought might get him to proverbial 'second base'? Despite her building attraction, the reporter in her now felt an even greater need to be sure. "What happens if you fail?"

His brow creased, and he looked away.

A long, almost painful, silence followed until he looked at her again.

"Then Joey has no chance at a cure at all."

"Nothing can be done?"

Lance shook his head. "Not at this moment. I want to change that."

As though a doctor were speaking, she felt the hopelessness. She could only imagine the frustration of the fight he waged. She reached out and squeezed his hand. "You shouldn't bear that burden alone."

"I'm not alone." His puckered brow released. "The families stand with me as do the geneticists working to find a cure and the staff dedicated to the research. We all fight for every dollar we can raise. I have a Finance Committee meeting next week, and I've invited Joey and his parents to testify. Saying no is hard when you stare into an afflicted person's eyes."

Kate nodded. "Which means…?"

"I could get an allocation."

A wave of emotions swept over Lance's face like an approaching sudden summer storm, and for a moment she could tell he struggled. But then his features smoothed into a mask hiding whatever he was thinking.

"Enough politics, would you like something to drink?" he asked. "The fridge has cold water, soft drinks, and assorted juices. We'll have to wait until we get to headquarters to actually get you some coffee."

"Cold water would be great." *Maybe it'll bring the temperature down a few degrees and help me breathe.*

Lance made the trip to the residential-size refrigerator and back in record time. As he handed her the bottled water, his thumb touched the side of her outstretched hand.

At the contact, she jerked backward, and the bottle fell from his hand. It rolled under the banquette and settled at her feet. Kate slid to the end of the bench seat and ducked under the table. "I'll get it."

"No, let me." Lance mirrored the move.

Beneath the table, their fingers tangled, and their gazes locked. The water bottle became secondary to the feel of his hand tightening around hers. Heat moved from her fingertips to her chest. Seeing Lance look at her lips and then into her eyes, she stilled, her heart racing. He wanted to kiss her, so she nodded her approval. Their hands released. Just as they started to right themselves, the RV bounced over a pothole. With a thud, the tops of their heads hit the bottom of the table. They looked at each other, and then at their tangled hands. Almost at the same time, they pulled back and sat up, the moment lost.

Kate rubbed the sore spot. "Well, that hurt." Worry clouded Lance's face.

"Let me get some ice." He slid across the bench seat, took two steps to the refrigerator and opened the freezer. "Sorry, none." He apologized with a shrug.

"I'll be fine." She noticed his grim expression. "Hey, it was just a little whack. Don't look so concerned. I'm not taking the U.S. Government to court for pain and suffering."

He returned to the bench. "I'm not worried about a lawsuit. I'm disappointed."

She detected regret in his voice. An intense desire to know if she was right rose inside her. "Why?"

He cupped her chin and skimmed his thumb across the ridge of her cheekbone. "We were about to have a moment."

Meeting his gaze, Kate saw how his pupils dilated with the touch and were now pools of deep blue. She let out one long breath. "Maybe we still can."

Lance dropped his hand and reached across the narrow space between them. "What do you think?"

The feel of his rough palm against hers was perilous, but she didn't care. Mesmerized, she watched his thumb make lazy circles across the back of her hand. His hand on hers felt like the most dangerous thing in the world but also the most inviting. For a second, she could not breathe. She looked up and caught his gaze. "I think we both want..." What on earth was she thinking? "I want to kiss you, but I'm thinking about how problematic that moment could be."

"You could be right." He leaned forward. "Maybe we should take this kissing thing slow."

The way his fresh, warm breath spilled over her lips made her pulse race. He smiled, revealing a small dimple, and her heart beat faster. "Slow is always good."

Lance didn't move away. Instead, he took her hand

and dropped a kiss on her knuckles.

Her heart did a little jump of contentment at his touch. "What are we doing?"

One dark eyebrow quirked. "For the moment holding hands."

She looked at their intertwined fingers. "I feel like I'm mishandling U.S. Government property."

"You aren't." Lance flashed another smile.

She took a deep breath but said nothing.

"Do you still want that water?" he whispered.

She put a hand on top of his and tightened her hold. "No."

"Are you sure?"

His voice was a low rasp. She lifted her chin and held his gaze. "Yes."

Their fingers twined. He left his side of the bench seat. "I like sitting here better." A quick smile darted across his face.

"I like you better on this side, too."

He centered his gaze on her lips. "I didn't expect to meet someone like you."

"Define *expect.*"

"Maybe expect is too strong a word." He looked at her hand and then into her eyes. "Truthfully, I didn't want to go to the reunion. I almost did the proverbial 'call in sick' thing." He laughed. "I'm glad I didn't because this moment wouldn't be happening."

Warmth rushed through Kate's veins like a speeding car. "What exactly *is* happening?"

He grinned. "This."

Before she could say a word, his mouth closed on hers. His kiss was light at first as it skimmed across her lips before growing more urgent. He drew back, and she met his gaze with an awareness both stunning and pleasing. He stared as if deciphering the meaning of the expressions fluttering across her face with each blink of her eyes.

"You're different than most women I know," he whispered.

She blew out a long breath of air. "Maybe a little, but I bet each and every one of them would be happy to be in my shoes right now." Her admission sent an arrow of desire shooting straight to her toes. She wanted him to kiss her again.

"I like your shoes right where there are." He curled a hand around the back of her neck. Keeping her close, he kissed her before pulling her into an undemanding embrace. He rested his cheek on hers. "When I'm around you, I can't think straight."

She lifted her hands and cradled his face. "That makes two of us." Kate struggled to dial back the physical response his nearness sparked.

He brushed his cheek against her temple. "Can we really do this?"

"Do what?" she asked after a few moments of breathless silence, her voice a whisper. She barely heard her question over the pounding of her racing heart.

"See each other. Start as friends and see what might develop."

"I'd like to but…" A huff of breath cut the rest of the sentence. She let her gaze roam his face. "Oh, heck. How hard could it be?" She leaned close and covered his mouth with hers.

No hesitation existed in her kiss and none in his, just a slow, thorough taking, moving her heartbeat to hyper-speed. The heat of building temptation singed away any thought of what she could do to him with one push of the Send button on her laptop. She curled her fingers on his shirt and pulled away from the kiss. She drew in a breath and slowly released it.

Lance cupped her jaw. "Kiss me once more like that and I won't have the willpower to turn back." The words came between light kisses. "I'll want to see you again and again and again." He smiled against her lips and then just as quickly frowned. "The next few weeks on the campaign trail are grueling. Not the greatest time to start a relationship." He pulled back. "Assuming you want one."

His throaty voice sounded more like a sigh. A slight upward tilt of her lips was tempered by an exhale. She tapped a forefinger on her cheek. "Let's see if I remember this correctly. Kiss me one more time like that…" She grabbed hold of Lance's hands and hauled him closer before kissing him as though she was sending him off to battle. After a few breathless moments, she pulled back. "Did I get that right?"

Lance opened his mouth to answer when the crackling of the intercom filled the air was suddenly followed by a tinny voice.

"Sir?"

Lance broke contact. "What?" he barked toward the speaker.

"We are arriving at headquarters."

Kate suddenly wished the partition was thicker. The driver's tone held a touch of amusement as though he knew what he was interrupting.

"I figured you would want to know."

The ambiance quickly moved from tender to

tension. The moment was gone. As the RV slowed, Kate was acutely conscious of the fleeting minutes remaining. Quickly, she ripped a corner from the campaign poster hanging on the left side of the large window and dug a pen from her purse. She scribbled her name and number on the tatter and handed the paper to Lance. "In case you need help during the campaign."

Lance tucked the piece into his shirt pocket. "You aren't coming to the office?"

She shook her head.

The bus stopped.

She glanced toward the door as it swung open. "I had fun tonight."

"Me, too." He stood and helped her slide from the banquette. "Funny, but I can't remember ever saying I enjoyed anything during campaign season." He took her hand. "Must be your fault." He looked at their joined hands and gave her a teasing grin. "I like you, Kate. I like you a lot."

Kate locked her gaze with his, and she felt as though she was falling into his eyes. "Senator Michaels, you are a very charming man underneath the party-political persona you don for public events."

For a breathless moment, they stared at each other, transfixed.

"Kate…" His fingers tightened around hers.

Kate closed her eyes. His touch felt too welcome, too exciting, and too right, but what she felt was also too wrong—for him and for her. She forced herself to smile, break contact, and walk toward the door. Putting a hand on the handle, she stopped. She didn't want her time with Lance to end, and she fought the urge to turn back. But she had other things to think about—her career, for one. She sucked in a deep breath as her pulse gave a traitorous leap with the guilt she felt. Her career wasn't the only one on the line. She held Lance's future in her hands. One story, one outrageous, misleading story and he could go down in flames.

But she was kidding herself if she thought two careers were all that was at stake. Everything she knew, everything she ever wanted, was on the line. Lance had gotten to her. She'd opened her heart, and now she was defenseless. She could play the game, but she couldn't win.

A maelstrom of emotions swept though her, like a sudden summer storm. When the end came, it wouldn't be a quiet break, and it certainly would be messy. When the dust settled, which one would be left standing?

Chapter Six

Kate sat cross-legged on her bed, looking at the blank laptop screen that should have held the words to the story due to Gartman by morning. She didn't want to write the copy he wanted her to write. She couldn't. As far as she could tell, Lance had no dark secrets.

Earlier, her reporter persona almost took up Lance's offer to tour his campaign office to get another invitation to meet staff and maybe hear some office gossip. Instead she went with her heart, collected her cars keys from Jack, and drove herself home.

Trapped between career and heart, she found herself in the devil-versus-the-angel-on-her-shoulders situation. Which one would win was still a toss-up. No doubt she was falling for Lance, but the Kate he wanted to know better was not real. Like an ironic role reversal, she was the smooth talker and Lance was the straight arrow. She could not imagine a resolution in which she and Lance could both emerge unscathed with their careers intact. Someone had to lose.

With a sigh, she entered her password and logged onto social media. She clicked on Lance's page. His profile picture, a posed camera shot, was his official congressional picture, but his smile held the same joy and his eyes the same light as when she was alone with him. Normally, she never let the subject of a story intrude on the assignment, but the more she got to know

Lance, the more distracted she became.

She skimmed through the latest entry. Too soon for Lance to have posted something personally, she assumed the political update was uploaded by his social media manager. She scrolled through the pictures, and her eyes widened and her mouth fell open when she reached the last one. The shot showed Lance talking to supporters, but in the background she clearly saw herself standing on the steps of his campaign bus. The entry already had four hundred views, seventy-five comments, and thirty shares. She scanned the page header. Lance had over thirty thousand followers. A sudden coldness hit her core. Holy heck. Social media is forever. Sooner or later, someone would see the shot, recognize her, and blow her cover in a comment.

She slammed closed the laptop and nearly rolled off the bed when she reached across the nightstand for her phone. "C'mon, c'mon," she coaxed. Each ring sounded like the toll of a countdown to doom. When the call finally connected, she almost screamed her greeting. "Susan, thank heavens you're home."

Susan greeted her with a yawn. "Home and in bed. What's up?"

"Remember my assignment?"

"You mean the reason you've been AWOL from the office for the last few days?"

"Very funny. I'm doing research and working." Kate parked the phone between her ear and shoulder and logged back onto social media. "I need you to help me with a little problem."

Susan sighed "Your problems are never little. Can it wait until morning?"

"I'll let you know in a minute." A few keystrokes

later, Kate groaned. The views climbed to over a thousand with double the comments and shares. "No, it can't wait. Is that tech guy you met a few weeks ago still around?"

"Yeah, why?"

"I need to remove a picture from a social media page." She felt like a social catfish, asking her friend to do something a bit contemptible, but at the moment, she could think of no other solution.

"You don't have a social media page."

Kate heard the hint of well-warranted wariness in Susan's voice. "Then obviously it isn't my page I want hacked." She sighed heavily. "A picture of me is on Senator Michaels' page."

Susan snickered. "You mean a picture of Kate Taylor is on his page. K. A. Stapleton would never have let down her guard enough to be photographed with a mark."

"A mark? I'm not an assassin." Maybe she was. A scandal could kill his political career. She bit her lower lip. "Can you make me disappear?" She heard a muffled expletive.

"Let me get this straight. You're asking me to have someone I barely know break into a U.S. Government-owned website to save your butt."

Confirmation came in a rush of breath. "Basically." The ensuing silence made Kate's room feel like the inside of a tomb. "Susan, are you still there?"

Susan huffed. "Are you oblivious to what happens to terrorists, hackers, and people who screw with the government?"

Kate forced a laugh. "You are none of those."

"And neither is my friend. The answer is no."

Kate's thoughts raced. Susan rarely changed her mind. "You haven't asked him. How do you know?"

"Because."

"Not an answer."

"You sound like my mother."

"Speaking of." Kate knew how to get Susan to bend the rules a little. "Does she know about your little adventure in Vegas? I'll bet your mom would love to learn she had a son-in-law for a week. If I recall, someone needed the name of a lawyer and a quick remedy for a hangover."

Susan sucked in a quick breath and released it. "You wouldn't."

"Not unless I am forced."

Susan sighed. "Removing the picture is that important?"

"It is." Kate could hear the change in Susan's tone. "And you're the only one who can help me now."

"I can't wait to hear why." She laughed. "Has to be a doozie of a tale."

"Now, you're laughing?"

"Sorry. But, oh what a tangled web we weave."

"The web is more than tangled," Kate admitted. "You know how tightly Gartman controls the media content. You have to catch him in the right mood to get new passwords. If your friend gets all patriotic and won't hack a government website, how about you ask him to log onto the social media page of *The Analytical* and replace my picture with…"

"You better not suggest using my picture."

"Would I ask you to do something creepy?" Kate grimaced. "Never mind, don't answer. Have him put up a gray silhouette like a few of the others on staff use."

"Why all the intrigue?"

"If you must know…"

Susan snickered. "If you want me to cover up whatever crime you committed, I must."

"I didn't commit a crime, and you are wasting time"

"Then I suggest you talk faster."

Kate let out a short breath of air. She had no choice. "A reporter at the town hall Lance held asked a question about Lance's apparent lack of female company and referenced the copy I wrote. I'm hoping nothing more comes up, but I can't be sure. He has a fact-checker who just might investigate me."

"So, it's Lance instead of Senator Michaels now."

Kate could picture the smug look on Susan's face. "He told his constituents he prefers to be casual and asked they call him by his surname instead of his title. Technically, I'm a constituent." She hoped Susan would accept the weak explanation.

"Okay, I'll give you that one, but even if I do a little sleight-of-hand with the picture, you can't stay hidden forever."

The tightness in Kate's stomach eased. Susan was about to cave. "I know. I just want to buy a little time to figure out what to do."

Susan fell silent for a moment. "Something tells me more is going on than I already know. Dish, girl. You are not the anonymous type."

Kate ran a hand through her hair. "I might have a situation." She could almost hear the gears in Susan's head spinning.

"No."

Susan made the word sound like five syllables.

"The whole assignment is getting complicated."

"Normally, I'd make you tell me everything but in this case, I don't want to know."

Kate's mind raced through possibilities. "You always want to know. Why not this time?"

"Because when the grand jury is impaneled, I can tell the truth." Susan paused for a moment. "Your Honor, I know nothing about any hacking."

Kate closed her eyes and dropped her head forward. "Just say you'll help." The ensuing laughter made her cringe.

"I won't ask my friend to break into the senator's social media page, but I will get him to take down your picture on *The Analytical*'s," Susan said. "But you owe me. Big time."

"And knowing I do scares me more than jail time." She disconnected the call before Susan could contest. She'd spent a lot of time convincing Susan to help. She hoped Susan wouldn't have a change of heart once she thought about what was asked.

****

The next day, Kate entered her cubicle and saw Gartman sitting on the edge of her desk, coffee mug in hand.

As soon as he saw her, he stood. "Stapleton. My office." He slammed his cup onto her desktop and left.

Susan peeked around the cubicle wall. "Only two reasons boss-man uses a voice that could turn back time—either you are Benson the Golden Boy, reporter god, walker-on-water, and he's about to pour a shot of the twelve-year-old scotch he keeps in his bottom desk drawer to celebrate something, or he's really angry."

Kate scowled. "Probably door number two." She

slid the trash can out from under her desk and grabbed a pen from the drawer. With the pen, she poked the coffee mug across the desktop until it dropped.

Susan nodded toward the trash. "I'd burn the cup." She wrinkled her nose. "The trash can and the pen, too," she added before disappearing behind the partition.

Kate released the pen and shook her hands. When she was satisfied every molecule of Gartman was gone, she tossed her purse into her bottom desk drawer and slowly walked to his office.

He barely glanced up. "Close the door and have a seat."

Kate sensed spotlights would be dropping from the ceiling and bathing her in an interrogation illumination as in clichéd detective serials of the '60s and '70s. Her thoughts raced. She decided to go on the offense. "Did you like the copy I sent last night?"

He locked his gaze with hers. "Dry and boring."

His expression was as vacant as the echo in his tone. Kate scrambled for a quick response. "I didn't think it was bad." His expression did not change. *Not a good sign.*

"I should have tweaked it more but didn't have time. I wanted the story up and live ASAP to cancel out the last piece of fluff you turned in."

Kate did not flinch. "I logged in. The piece had more hits than the first one. A good sign, right?"

"Hits, yes. Comments, no. The lack of feedback tells me people aren't interested. Maybe I should take you off the assignment and get Benson to finish."

Think, Kate. I can't let that fiction-writing vulture destroy Lance's career in four columns. "No need. I have a plan."

Gartman crossed his arms over his chest and leaned back. "Better be a good one. A campaign season moves fast , and a tell-all needs time to cook."

She already regretted what she was about to say. "If you look on the senator's social media page, you'll see my picture. I'm making inroads." She could see interest dart around his face and was already filled with guilt for the duplicity she would have to carry out to save the assignment. "I'll have something soon."

"How soon?" He sat forward and slid his arms onto the desk top. "I don't wait well."

Don't I know it? "Trust me."

He glowered. "For the moment, I don't have a choice." With a flick of the wrist, he waved her out. She walked to the door and turned. Gartman's gaze was fixed on his computer screen. She would bet a week's pay he was about to add his name to the senator's social media followers and check the picture she just mentioned. He never left anything to chance.

As she strode to her cubicle, she could hear loud banging coming from Susan's side. She peeked in and saw Susan whacking her keyboard. "You could get arrested for assault."

Susan shook her head. "Naw. I think jelly is under the m-key. It's stuck."

"Shut down before you break something."

"Why?"

She pulled Susan's chair from the desk. "Because you're with me today."

Susan hesitated for a moment then powered off. "Where am I going?"

"We," Kate emphasized, "are about to volunteer."

She saw the guarded look in Susan's eyes. "Remember how we always said we wanted to do something civic-minded someday? Well, today is the day. We're campaign workers."

****

Susan eased her car into the only space in front of an office just beyond the shops on the main Princeton shopping drag. "I can't believe we are actually infiltrating a campaign office."

Kate was already out of the car and feeding the parking meter. "What did you say?"

"I said I feel like a double agent." She grinned. "But I like it." She looked up and down the street. "Which way?"

Kate headed to the left. "How can you miss the balloons and the signs? No one has a birthday party on the streets of downtown Princeton."

Susan got in step beside her. "I do love a good adventure." At the door to the building, she skidded to a stop. "OMG." Her gaze fixed on the bigger-than-life picture of Lance Michaels adorning the front window.

"Yes, that's him," Kate looked at her jaw-dropped friend.

Susan walked to the poster. "You go inside. I'll be out here drooling for a few minutes."

Kate laughed. "I'll tell the senator you said 'hi'."

Hours later, Kate flexed her fingers. Her whole hand was stiff from peeling pre-addressed labels from sheets and sticking them onto #10 envelopes. As soon as she found out Lance wasn't in town, Susan left. One of the workers told her Lance was in D.C. at a voting session but was expected back over the weekend to attend a fundraiser. Kate didn't want to raise suspicion by walking in and walking out, so to entrench herself in the campaign workers' good graces, she offered to finish the last few sheets of address labels.

The volunteer left about an hour ago, and with the last flyer addressed, Kate stood and tossed the empty label sheet into the trash. She walked to the rear office and dug her cell phone from her purse to open the app for the car service she occasionally used when she heard the front door open and close. She disconnected the call. "Forget something?"

"Yes, to let someone know I was coming," Lance shouted back.

Kate almost ran to the front room. Her heart jumped when she saw him standing near the first desk, a cardboard beverage carrier in one hand and a white bakery bag in the other. The wonderful aroma of coffee filled the room. She pointed. "If one of those is decaf, I'll take it."

He slipped the carrier on the desk and checked the writing on the side of the coffee cups. "I'm surprised you're here, Kate."

"You shouldn't be. The election is looming, and I said I'd help."

He handed her the third cup. "Decaf. The milk is in the fridge in the back."

"Black is fine." A muscle twitched at the corner of her mouth. She pressed her lips together to control the grin. Not wanting Lance to know how excited she felt seeing him, she took a sip of coffee before saying anything. The coffee was old, cold, and bitter, but it gave her the opportunity to calm her racing heart. "Aren't you supposed to be in D.C. voting on something?"

"The bill was tabled." Lance picked up the bakery bag and poked around inside. "Bear claw?"

"You mean five pounds on my hips." She lifted her chin. "Is anything there that's a bit less dense?"

Lance raised the bag and jiggled it. "Nope. The coffee shop didn't have much left." Leaning forward, he opened the bag and held it out. "How about we share?"

"Two and a half pounds each?"

"Deal."

She could not tear her gaze from his face. Though Lance kept the conversation light, his eyes were unrelenting in their intensity. Mesmerized by his sensual mouth and wicked dimples, she nearly dropped the pastry she chose. He made her want to forget everything.

His chest expanded with a deep breath. "I'll get milk from the small kitchen in the back, while you clean off a desktop for our carb-fest."

As she pushed papers and flyers to the edge of the desk, she grinned, lightness settling in her chest with the thought of being alone with Lance. By sheer will, she controlled any response he might notice. The more time she spend with Lance, the more she wanted both him and her career but once she finished her assignment or told him the truth, she might not have either. They'd part ways—she back to her cubicle writing stories of celebrity numbness, and Lance to D.C. if she hadn't destroyed his career. She sat in a worn desk chair and sighed. A sensation she recognized as regret tickled her stomach. She ordered away the feeling. She had a job to do.

Lance returned carrying a half empty gallon of

milk and some paper towels. He arched an eyebrow and sank into a folding chair next to her. "I thought you hated politics."

"At this moment, not so much." Fearing he'd see the joy in her eyes, she dropped her gaze. She flexed her fingers a few times. "But envelope stuffing should be considered an extreme sport."

Lance set down his coffee mug. "Hand sore?"

She rubbed the knuckles on the back of her right hand. "My fingers are killing me from pasting address labels on flyers with your face."

"Wait here." He stood and disappeared down the hallway.

One last irresistible tinge of optimism bubbled upward and erupted before Kate could stop it. "I'm not going anywhere for the moment. No ride."

He stepped into view. His eyebrows drew together. "No car?"

Even at a distance, she could see the puzzled look on his face. Why in the world had she told him she had no way home? A small smile curved her mouth. She knew exactly why. Her hormones flipped her emotion switch from reporting to flirting, and she wanted him to drive her home. "Long story."

"I'll take you home, and you can fill me in on the way."

She swore she heard delight in his voice and was glad he ducked back into the kitchen, otherwise her broad smile might be something else she would have to explain.

Lance returned with a dish towel. He sat across from her and held out his hand.

Kate hesitated. "What's your plan?"

He held the towel like a hammock. "Can't have one of my helpers hurting on my account. I find a nice warm towel relaxes tired muscles." His gaze followed water droplets to the floor. "Warm and maybe a bit too wet."

She extended both hands. "Doesn't matter. I'm so in."

He wrapped the towel around her left hand and skated his chair closer.

Inhaling, she caught a hint of citrus and musk. The pleasant scent shifted her thoughts to the day she met him, and temptation flared. Conflicted, she stared at the man she'd grown to like more than she dared. Not the stereotypical politician she imagined, he was intense about his calling but with a gentle kindness and a sincere wish to help that made him unique. Not to mention he was utterly masculine and very easy on the eyes.

Abruptly, she looked away. For Pete's sake, what was she thinking? The hole she found herself in only seemed deeper. His job was to campaign and win another term, and hers was to possibly destroy any chance he might have by writing an explosive series of editorials. Besides, even if she didn't complete her assignment, once re-elected he'd be absorbed by Capitol Hill, leaving his New Jersey District Offices to his local congressional staff.

Like a deflating balloon, all the happiness she felt when she first saw him drained. She couldn't win. She pushed away the disappointing thought.

He manipulated the fabric wrapped around her hand.

As the warmth spread into her skin, she shut her

eyes and focused on the lessening pain in her fingers not the man.

After a few minutes, he pulled free the towel and tossed it onto the desktop. He took her hand between his and rubbed his thumbs across the skin below her knuckles while his fingers caressed her palm.

She sighed. "That feels so good." When the pressure increased, she flinched.

"No pain, no gain," he said.

Kate opened her eyes. "Whatever you say."

"Whatever I say?" He raised one eyebrow. "Are you sure?" He shot her a wide smile.

The expression on his face told her he might want to explore something more than campaign literature stuffing. She cocked her head to one side. Was a suppressed D.C. ego finally surfacing? "Whatever you say, within the scope of your campaign and the laws of decency."

Lance chuckled.

The gaze meeting hers glinted with amusement.

"I have never met a woman like you," Lance said.

She lowered her brows. A tingling settled in her chest, and her breathing deepened. "And what kind of woman might I be?"

"An enigma. You look so open to anything, yet underneath, I sense a will of pure steel. You don't adjust what you believe to a situation."

His words flattered her. He sounded like a politician who didn't consider her just a vote. For a moment briefer than a heartbeat, she nearly let down her guard and shoved aside the growing thought Lance could be different than the stereotypical D.C. politician portrayed in daily media stories. "But you hardly know me."

"I know more than you think."

"Such as?"

"I know you're left-handed."

"How so?" She didn't remember doing anything particularly lefty.

"Because I pay attention. You held your drink in your left hand at the reunion, and you grabbed the glad-hand on the side of the RV door for support with your left hand before you started up the steps. You had to be using your dominant hand."

Kate nodded. "I guess I better be careful you don't uncover any more of my secrets." *Especially the one that might ruin your career.* Only the smile she held disguised how much she questioned her motives.

After a few minutes of massage, Lance took her other hand and gave it the same restless attention. "Feel better?"

"Uh-huh." She tipped back her head and surrendered to the ripples of enjoyment moving knuckles to elbow. She lowered her chin. "Reaching across the table can't be very comfortable." She glanced to her left. "Scoot over to my side."

He kept a hand on hers when he slid around his chair. "We hold hands a lot lately."

Feeling happier than she ever had, she looked into his smile. He was perfect. Though the notion seemed ridiculous under the circumstances, she knew he could change her if she let him. "Seems so."

"I like that we do."

Kate stared at their intertwined hands but did not respond.

Lance slid closer. "Kate?"

She looked up. He was near enough for her to see his dilated pupils against the dark blue of his eyes. "Yes?"

"I want to kiss you."

Her pulse hammered. She wanted that kiss, but a shard of doubt pierced her. Kissing him would again take her across the line separating reporting on Lance from getting involved with him. Could she continue, knowing any relationship they might explore began with a lie? When he moved closer his muscled arm slid around her back, and a bolt of heat leapt through her melting her doubts. Of course, she could juggle both. "Then what are you waiting for?" She held her breath.

A frown creased his forehead. "The war inside my head to stop. My situation is very complicated at the moment. Are you ready for what could be a very bumpy ride?"

Her pulse thudded as reality kicked in. Lance wasn't a political player jumping on the chance for a little action. Why did he have to be so perfect? She pressed her lips together and nodded. "I can handle the challenge."

"Are you certain? Because I want you in my life."

She let out a long breath and put a forefinger across his lips, holding back a reaction to the jolt she felt. "Are *you* certain anything between us should even happen?" she asked. "We are very different people."

"Because you sell toilet ads and I work in government?"

"Among other things." The half-lie did nothing to assuage her rising guilt.

He chuckled. "You're not holding back anything I should know such as being a foreign operative, are you?"

"No." She drew out the word. *Working as a spy would be easier to explain.* "Nothing like that." She saw his eyes shadow with an emotion she did not recognize.

"I believe being honest is the right thing to do." His voice lowered. "Especially in a relationship."

Relationship? The word hit her between the eyes and rattled around her brain. Right now, she didn't need a relationship. She needed a confessional. Squinting, she gestured between the two of them. "You think we are in a relationship?"

"The early stages at least," he said. He lifted his chin and winked.

The lack of hesitation in his voice indicated he was sincere. As if caught in a Cat 5 hurricane, red flags battered her mind, and she grabbed on to some retreating prudence. *Slow this down, Kate. Take charge.* "We hardly know each other."

His features relaxed. "We can find out more together."

Lance's smile accented his dimples and the gleam in his dark eyes. When he pulled her to standing, she caved. A day, a week, a month—whatever they could have, she'd take it. She had never made such a quick and complete connection with any man like the one with Lance. This strange, instant, but unquestionably fascinating attraction was something she wanted to explore. She clutched his shoulders. She'd give him one chance to walk away. "We could be a disaster in the making."

Grinning, he brushed a stray lock of hair from her forehead and raised a brow. "Or we could be something great."

She could feel her heart drum and suspected the rapid beat had more to do with anticipation than with doubt. She leaned forward and lightly kissed the edge of his smile before nuzzling her cheek against his. "Look out, world," she whispered against his skin.

She trailed her lips to his, instantly transporting her to a swirling void where consequences did not matter. Nothing was relevant but the taste of Lance's kisses and the feel of his arms around her. None of the doubts and uncertainties plaguing her only minutes before had a place now. Only warmth, wild emotion, and Lance existed.

When he nibbled on her lower lip, she clutched his shoulders, the restless friction of her fingers against the fine cotton of his shirt only adding to the sensations taking over each of her senses. She didn't stop to think but simply unleashed her building emotion and let her kisses go wild. Lance slanted his mouth against hers with a reckless abandon she would never associate with the calm, professional façade he presented to the world.

Lordy, this guy could kiss.

A groan burst from her, and she lost herself in the waves of heat and turbulence assailing her senses. Her head spun, and she pulled back, forcing him to slow. He slid his lips over her cheek before trailing kisses across her neck. Then suddenly everything stopped.

Lance straightened and raked an unsteady hand through the dark hair that had fallen onto his face. He locked his gaze with hers.

She saw dazed emotion in his eyes. "What's wrong?" Her voice sounded husky.

He sucked in a deep lungful of air. "We haven't

even had a first date, and I was thinking about getting to at least second base." He lifted his head and met her gaze. "That's no way to treat a lady."

A fragment of sound somewhere between laughter and disappointment escaped her. "I don't think a lady would have kissed you the way I did, so we're about even."

Lance took a step away. He lifted his head, and their gazes met. For a long moment, neither spoke.

Kate stared at the sexy way Lance's hair had been transformed from perfectly styled to touchably messy. She needed to figure out what made her want to toss out everything she knew and throw herself into his arms. Until then, she couldn't afford to let him find out the truth about the way she felt.

She nearly laughed out loud. Truth? In her line of work? Tabloid journalism was about as far from the truth as the earth was from the moon. The only saving grace would be when Lance inevitably learned she was a fraud, she'd at least some wonderful memories to cherish in the cardboard box under the bridge in which she lived after spending all her money defending herself in the lawsuit he was sure to file.

"It's late." She touched his cheek, enjoying the scrape of the emerging stubble. "I could use that ride home now."

He smiled. "Done."

She dropped her hand. "Will you be in town all weekend?"

He shook his head. "Tomorrow only. I need to be back in D.C. on Sunday."

Kate suddenly felt alone. "So soon?"

"A Senate Bill is coming out of committee, and I

need to review the wording. I'm sure the Senate President is re-scheduling the voting session as we speak, but I can't be sure." He turned and retrieved his jacket from the next desk.

The back he presented looked rigid, as though he grappled with thought. "Work always wins." She hoped he did not catch the disappointment in her voice when she realized she was also talking about herself.

"But I would like a real first date sometime soon."

Kate placed a hand on his arm, the connection making her tingle. She knew her smile would give away her answer, but she didn't care. "I was afraid you wouldn't ask."

Chapter Seven

After dropping Kate at home, Lance pulled the car to the curb about a block away. He couldn't concentrate on driving. His mind was a muddled pool of conflicting thoughts. He hadn't expected such swift and sudden attraction. He'd almost lost it—and with a woman he barely knew. Up to now he carefully controlled his feelings, but he could sense the balance shifting.

A woman like Kate could be as dangerous as she could be provocative. For six years, he carefully protected his reputation, dating but not getting overly involved with any woman. But Kate intrigued him. A sensual stranger, she tossed aside the cool, ad-selling professional he met at his class reunion and let loose a woman who knew exactly what she wanted from a man. He responded like a man in need but was left wanting something more permanent.

Could he find a way to have a solid relationship with Kate and still keep the campaign from turning into a Q&A about his love life? The media loved romance and scandal. More important, could she handle a fish-bowl existence when the press found out about her? For the first time since he met Kate, doubt about the future assailed him.

Kate was a political rookie, a babe in arms for the D.C. press to chew up and spit out if a reporter thought a story about her would get a lead on the evening news.

Could she handle that kind of deep scrutiny? Did he even want to ask her to try? Over the years, he had watched even the most seasoned Washington socialite crumble under the constant analysis of the political press. More than one congressional career ended in early retirement or on a court floor because of a relationship gone wrong. Not that he suspected Kate was the same as women who grabbed onto powerful men for the laurels of the catch, but he was savvy enough to realize she might have secrets. Heck, he had a few of his own. Only by the Grace of God had none surfaced yet.

Away from the Beltway, perhaps they'd share those secrets in time, after he earned her trust, and she earned his. Trust was not a normal part of the D.C. lifestyle and not something that came easily. He raked a hand through his hair. Had he become so jaded he was already judging her without cause? He shook his head. He would not allow dogmatic political cancer to claim him the way it claimed many of his colleagues.

He gripped the steering wheel with both hands and laughed, remembering how they met. Not at a political fundraiser, not with a letter of introduction from some high-ranking lobbyist, but at something as benign as a class reunion. There, she put him on notice she was not the proverbial side-chick who wanted a tour of the White House and an apartment with a view of the Capitol. Suddenly having a relationship was no longer a choice between wanting someone to share his life or a career with another six years of being cautious and alone. He wanted both. The last thing he ever expected happened at possibly the worst possible time. Kate Taylor was becoming more important than the idea of another empty, game-playing six years on the Hill.

He started the car and began the drive to his home in Lawrenceville. The upcoming campaign season was looking pretty good—win or lose.

When he realized he didn't remember a life outside Washington, his elation suddenly turned to apprehension. Six years in government was as fulfilling as it was addicting. Could he handle life as a lobbyist or just another has-been speaker on the college campus circuit? Could he adjust if he lost the coming election? And if he lost, would he blame himself solely for the defeat or would that burden also include one big distraction named Kate? He took a deep breath and let it out slowly. Right now, he could not say for sure he had that answer.

****

With no one normally in the office on a Saturday, Kate thought she'd quickly file her next story and grab a few things from her desk, but Gartman's and Benson's cars were in the parking lot. A coincidence? She didn't think so.

She found Benson sitting on the edge of her desk holding a manila file folder. She didn't need to read the label to know the folder held all her notes on Lance.

Benson barely acknowledged her with a nod.

She ran to him and snatched the file. "Find anything interesting?" The acid lacing her voice would have left deep scars on anyone else, but Benson did not react. She slid the file into the left file drawer, retrieved the key from her purse, and locked the desk. Then, just to make a point, she dropped the key into her bra with enough drama to earn her an acting award nomination.

Benson scowled. "I could file a sexual harassment

charge against you for that gesture."

A smirk moved over her lips. She pushed his button. "Or I could file one against you if you try to get that key." She crossed her arms over her chest.

He rolled his eyes. "Don't flatter yourself."

Kate brushed off the comment with a manufactured laugh and a twisted smile. "You're kidding, right?"

"Oh, for God's sake."

"For *your* sake, I'd like to know why I caught you ransacking my desk. Insecurity, perhaps?" A flush crept across Benson's cheeks.

"I wanted to be sure you're not in over your head with the Michaels assignment."

By sheer force of will, Kate controlled the sneer trying to curl on her lips. "And how does your going through my desk ensure my wellbeing?" Benson opened his mouth, but she cut any words he might utter with a wave of her hand. "Don't humiliate yourself by trying to answer." A shiver of disgust ran down her spine. "I know what you are doing. I'm fully capable of getting this story by myself."

He shook his head. "I read your last two articles. Good, but not great. You're supposed to find dirt. I read fluff."

Guilt spread like wildfire through her blood stream. She lifted her chin. "I don't have to explain my assignment."

Benson made a tsking sound. "The assignment probably should have gone to someone more professional."

"I *am* a professional." He was positioning himself to take over. If he did, he would destroy Lance. Her stomach heaved. She couldn't let that happen and hoped she didn't look as sick as she felt.

"Not that I can see. Maybe you need some help."

Kate surged forward. "I've been working on angles for two weeks. I don't need any help from someone who obviously wants in on my story." She glanced to the top desk drawer for emphasis and saw his expression harden. She crossed her arms. "Why are you here on a Saturday anyway?"

Benson shot her a smug look. "Business."

She pointed to the desk drawer. "Monkey business."

Benson jerked back. "That's no way to talk to a coworker."

Kate shifted her gaze to Gartman's office before settling it on Benson's face like a laser on a target. "Co-conspirator is a better word."

He feigned hurt with a hand to his chest. "I am shocked you think that." He leaned forward, gripped the edge of the desk with both hands, and shifted toward her. "Especially with the cherry assignment you were given over me, which if you ask me, isn't going so well."

She wanted to slap his self-righteous smirk into the next cubicle. "No one asked you."

"I could give you a hand, and we could knock this piece out of the park together."

His forced smile disgusted Kate. "Really?" She drew out the word as a sour taste filled her mouth.

"I've been known to break a story or two. We could collaborate and share the byline." He winked. "And maybe win an award or two."

Was she imagining things, or did he look like he was about to salivate at the thought of ruining Lance's political career? She shook her head. "No thanks. I'm good."

"I'm willing to give you some pointers."

Or you can go away and polish your plaques and leave me alone. Irritation rose. Benson's ego was bigger than anyone she had ever met. He was a master at pushing co-workers to the brink, and she was in the crosshairs. She had to give him the proverbial dust-off and still let him think he had a chance at the story so he would leave. Despite the disgust she felt, she managed a smile. "If I get into a jam, I'll be sure to call."

The grin on his face came instantaneously. "I'll be expecting one."

Fortunately, or unfortunately depending on the point of view, Gartman appeared in the hallway. His presence dissuaded Kate from grabbing the nearest object from her desk and sending it toward Benson's head.

"Stapleton! My office! Now!" Gartman beckoned with a crook of a forefinger.

The irritation in Gartman's voice snaked down Kate's spine, but she refused to react. As Gartman's footsteps faded, she reinforced her fortitude and gathered her things. "No sense waiting around. I can find my way to the boss' office on my own." She stared at Benson and waited.

Benson blinked. "I'll be in touch then."

"Don't bother." She waggled her fingers. "Bye." She walked away before the curse forming on her lips became audible.

Gartman groused as soon as she entered his office. "What the heck are you thinking?" He pointed to the pictures strewn on the desktop. "These shots look like you and your target are getting pretty cozy, and not in a fact-finding way." He stared at Kate and waited.

Kate leaned forward and glanced at the photos. With a forefinger, she repositioned a few. "I'm gaining his trust." She slowly lifted her gaze to Gartman's and hoped the guilt bubbling in her gut did not show in her eyes. "I just need a bit more time to spring the trap." She had no plan to trick Lance. What a fraud she was becoming. For a split second, she thought she might throw up.

Gartman gathered the pictures into an even stack and stashed them in the top desk drawer. "Time's running out. The election is in three weeks. I'm moving up the deadline for a bombshell to the weekend. Can you handle it?"

Kate started and slowly nodded. "But this assignment isn't exactly like covering an annual county fair. Building a tell-all takes time. I have to check facts."

Gartman waved her off. "Forget the facts. I need juice. Give me something to have *The Analytical* bursting with new followers."

She held her gaze level and steady. "Ah, ever look up the definition of defamation?"

"Retractions to cover that are a one-inch note on the last page a month after the story breaks."

Fuming, she let out a short breath. "No one reads retractions."

"I need vendors to buy online ads, not read retractions." Gartman jabbed a pointy finger in her direction. "You get me some something juicy by next weekend or…"

Kate lost the control she'd been struggling to

contain. As she leaned forward, both palms hit the desk with a loud whack. "Or what? You'll let Benson loose?" A shiver of revulsion ran along her spine. "The man has no scruples. He's the king of fake news."

"But he has the readership."

"What about a man's career?"

"Michaels will be just fine." Gartman scoffed. "He'll end up on the lecture circuit like all disgraced politicians."

Kate gritted her teeth so hard her jaw hurt. Gartman sounded like he already had a piece written just in case. To him, building a readership was worth destroying a man's career. She had to figure out how to do the first *and* protect Lance from the second. She sighed, more out of culpability than anything else. "I'll get you a story. A real story. One based on real facts."

Gartman rolled his eyes. "Stories in broadsheets are more based in conjecture rather than fact. You've written enough rumor-based copy to know how things work in this business."

"On celebrities who don't care much about anything but themselves," she quickly justified. "Not someone who cares about this country and its citizens."

He laughed. "Going all red, white, and blue on me?"

She forced herself to stay calm. *I have to stop this witch hunt.* "I'll find an angle you'll love."

He picked up the picture of Kate getting into the campaign bus and held it out. "Use this for inspiration."

With an angry huff, she snatched the photo from his hand. "Senator Michaels uses the RV to go from campaign stop to campaign stop. Sometimes, he has three or four stops in a day."

"Then use that angle."

"You can't be serious." She stared blankly at him. She wasn't certain, but Gartman appeared to be licking his lips at what formed inside his scheming brain.

"What's the matter with you? Is dogging that guy messing with your brain? Here's your headline— Campaign Bus or Love Shack? You decide."

Gartman's voice was heavy with impatience. Kate blinked furiously, determined he wouldn't see how disgusted his headline made her. "That suggestion is sick."

"No. It's an eye-catcher." Gartman leaned back in his leather desk chair and folded his hands across his stomach. "Genius."

"Reckless," Kate countered.

"By now, I assumed you understood the finer points connected to the job of a tabloid journalist." Gartman raised an eyebrow. "Was I wrong?"

Kate's stomach heaved. She was trapped, but she refused to let him see her squirm. "I know what I need to do."

Gartman pointed to the door. "Then I need copy sent to my inbox by tomorrow morning."

Pushing her chair back, her stomach lurching, Kate locked her gaze with his. A burst of exasperated air escaped her. "It will be there."

He waggled four fingers in the air. "I'll be waiting."

She stormed out of his office and banged shut the door. His laughter followed her.

Outside, she stopped and stiff-armed her palm against the wall to steady her shaking knees. He'd gotten the best of her. She hated how she let down her guard. Her mind spun with warring thoughts. To buffer Lance, she had to keep her job, but to keep her job, she had to write trash copy. How could she keep fact from crossing over to fiction without losing herself in the process?

****

A few hours after the confrontation with Gartman and Benson, Kate pulled into Susan's driveway and honked.

Susan opened the front door, gave her the 'in-a-minute' sign, and disappeared back inside.

Kate needed more than a minute to pull together her scattered thoughts. She felt more like a spy than a journalist and almost canceled the hurry-up plans to grab Susan and head for Lance's campaign office. She couldn't stop now. She was in too deep, maybe even way over her head.

Closing her eyes, she leaned back against the headrest. She had a lot to think about before she sent copy to Gartman, but the only thing she could think about was what she had to do to Lance. She wouldn't call what they had a relationship just yet, but it was close. She didn't love him. Not yet. But she did like being with him. He was funny and sensitive, occasionally a bit too serious, but not enough to make her want to cut the time together short.

She knew her attraction didn't stop at his inner attributes. He was also sexy...incredibly sexy. Lordy, when he kissed her, even just held her hand, the feelings he kindled made her think of things she had not thought about in years. An attraction so strong could only lead to one thing in the tangled web she wove—someone would lose, and she wasn't quite ready to admit it might be her.

When she heard the passenger door open, she snapped open her eyes. "Hey, Sues. Ready to go undercover?"

Susan buckled in. "Do I have a choice?"

Kate put the car in reverse and backed out. "No."

Susan popped on her sunglasses. "People at the office are asking about you and the senator. You know the staff reads every story. Gartman practically requires a book report. Chatter is you watered down the copy." She looked at Kate. "What gives?"

The gossip machine was cranking. Kate stared straight ahead. "I've turned in two articles."

"And they were kind of white bread for tabloid reporting."

"Really?" Kate glanced at Susan. "The first one got a little play."

"But you backed off on the second."

Even Susan knew the article was fluff. She avoided Susan's questioning gaze. "This time tabloid journalism is not as simple as turning in a story telling adoring fans another celebrity is cheating on his or her significant other. This particular assignment could affect the fate of the free world."

A scoffing sounded from the passenger seat. "I know you don't really think that."

Kate sighed. "No."

Susan settled back. "Watch yourself, because once the office grapevine finishes spreading trash talk in the building, the stink will spread outside."

Kate's stomach clenched with concern. "What else is being said?"

"According to the smack talk, you spent a lot of

time alone in a back room with Senator Michaels the day of the reunion."

For a long moment, silence filled the car as Kate wondered how anyone at the office knew. Searching for the right words, she drew in a deep breath. "I did. We had a meeting in a small kitchen office with security watching my every move."

Susan slid her glasses down her nose and looked at Kate over the rim. "And you didn't tell me?"

Kate waved off the question. "It was no biggie. I was working, remember?" She gripped the steering wheel tighter. Gossip was like that child's telephone game. What starts as a simple comment turns into a fiction novel after a few repeats. "What else?"

"The word is you make sure everyone leaves campaign headquarters so you two can do the ooh-la-la on one of the desks."

Grateful no other car was in sight, Kate slammed on the brakes. She made sure she held Susan's gaze. "Not true!"

"No need to pop a wheelie." Susan recovered her purse from the floor. "That's exactly what I told staff, but you know, in our line of work…" She shrugged.

"Say no more." Kate started driving again. Both angered and horrified, she knew about gossip snowballs rolling down hills. She often pushed one off a cliff herself to juice up a story. Now, when she was just realizing how wrong it was to color the facts, and she was in it up to her eyeballs. Her stomach turned to mush. How much longer could she separate her job from her—her what? Her heart? The walls closed in, and she gave her head a small shake then realized Susan was still talking. 'Sorry, Sues. I know you're trying to help. I'll keep everything you said in mind."

"Okay, but what will you do when this is all over? One way or another, Senator Michaels will move on after the election, and, unless you don't deliver the blockbuster story Gartman expects, you'll still be working at *The Analytical.*"

Kate cut her gaze to Susan. "Thanks for all the faith you have in my reporting."

"Reporting?" Susan snorted a laugh as Kate turned right and headed toward Princeton. "That word is a stretch for work we do." She checked her make-up in the visor mirror and wiped away some errant eyeliner with her forefinger. "Not that the fact you two getting cuddly is a bad thing."

Kate's palms became moist. "We are not getting cuddly." She grabbed sunglasses from the built-in holder atop the rearview mirror and jammed them onto her face so Susan would not see the lie in her eyes. "I am developing a bond so I can do my job."

Susan snickered. "A bond? Is that what they call it these days?"

Kate glanced at her then looked away without answering.

"Okay, you don't want to talk." Susan settled into the seat. "But you will, and when you do, you'll need someone you trust to listen. I just want you to know I'm here for you."

Kate answered with a small nod.

"By the way, where are we going? Your text message, though it sounded extremely urgent, you forgot to include the old reporter who-what-when-where and why."

Dryness assaulted her mouth as though she just

drank a cup of sand. "We're off to the senator's campaign office. A big mailing needs to be postmarked today. Remember, we are volunteers."

Susan laughed. "The cuddly place."

"Don't even," Kate said from behind clenched teeth.

Susan flinched. "I was only trying to break the tension."

"Try a knock-knock joke. But speaking of cuddly, did you know Gartman and Benson had a meeting at the office today?"

Susan smacked her thighs with her palms. "Benson never does Saturdays."

"I know. That's why I'm concerned."

"You think he might undermine your assignment?"

"They aren't exactly having a bromance. Gartman hates Benson but won't admit it because Benson's style of fiction-journalism brings in subscriptions."

Susan muttered a broken cussword. "And unfortunately, Benson thinks the mainstream media might come knocking any minute, so he isn't going anywhere anytime soon." She lifted her chin. "What's your plan?"

Kate sucked in a deep breath then expelled the words like a machine gun. "I don't have one." Her dad always told her when you are in a hole stop digging. Why did she feel as though she just picked up a bigger shovel? If hell existed, she was in one of her own making. Tabloid journalism boiled down to survival of the fittest. She didn't dare back out.

At the stop light, she slid the sunglasses onto her head and glanced at her reflection in the rearview mirror. Her eyes looked black, and she wondered if they reflected her soul. Suddenly, she didn't like the person she was becoming.

****

In the lot behind Lance's campaign headquarters, Susan unbuckled her seatbelt even before Kate shifted her car to park. "I forgot to mention Finley's meeting me here."

Kate turned off the engine. "Who is Finley?" She walked to the rear entrance and opened the door.

"Covert operations come with a price, and the price to erase your image from the website was dinner with the nerd guy." Susan stepped inside. "You know I don't speak teckkie." She rolled her eyes. "It is going to be a very long dinner."

"I owe you." Kate knew the payback would be huge. "Be gentle when you collect."

Susan shrugged. "Hey, he could invent the next big computer game. I'm keeping an open mind." She laughed. "He's picking me up at four, so let's get this clandestine info-grab started."

As soon as she entered the campaign office, Kate locked her gaze on Lance. His back to her, he bent over a desk, scanning the laptop in front of one of the volunteers. When he reached across the desk and picked up a file folder, she could see his shirt sleeves were rolled up to his elbows, and he wore no tie. He had apparently been here for some time.

Ken Adams, Lance's local Chief of Staff, spotted Kate and Susan as he walked by with a roll of campaign stickers. "Welcome back."

"Ready to work," Kate announced.

"But out of uniform." He peeled two labels from the roll and extended them.

Kate placed one 'Re-elect Lance Michaels' label on her shirt and handed the other to Susan who stuck it on her hip. "What do you need us to do?"

Adams pointed down the hallway. "Phone bank is in the office to the right. I need one of you to help with calling partisan voters and reminding them to vote. The senator can't win if the voters don't show up."

"Out of sight and talking. Perfect for me," Susan headed to the phone bank.

Kate walked with Adams to a folding table littered with fliers.

"I need someone to separate these into issues germane to the towns in the senator's districts and slap on the address labels."

Kate held out her hand and nodded. "I'm your girl."

"I hope not."

Lance's rebuttal came from behind her. She held her breath and turned. "His girl in a working sense, of course." She pumped her fist. "Ready to get you re-elected, I mean."

Lance handed Adams the file folder. "Can you check these voter registrations?"

Adams nodded and walked off.

Lance gestured toward the table. "What did he want you to do with these?"

She looked at the tabletop, mostly to break the connection she felt looking into his eyes. "Sort and address."

He winked. "Sounds like another hand massage in the making." He glanced around the busy room and then at his watch. "I have a better option. Twenty or so workers are here, and it is well past lunch. I could use some help making a food run. Are you up for assisting me?"

Not wanting to appear as eager as she felt, she hid her smile. "Then I am *your* girl."

He touched her hand. "I wish you were," he whispered.

She wasn't sure she heard him right and cocked her head to one side. "What?"

"I wish…" His lips thinned. "Never mind." He slid a hand to the small of her back. "Hungry volunteers might not come back." At the rear door, he stopped. "Late lunch run," he called out to a few people at a small table placing address labels on postcards. "Be right back."

The hand on her back slid to hold onto hers as they walked to the parking lot. She turned to meet Lance's gaze and smiled. What about him made her defenses drop? The building attraction she felt every time she was with him was getting more dangerous.

As they walked toward his car, a gust of wind kicked up, and she was surrounded by his musky scent. The enjoyable aroma brought an awareness followed closely by a sense of the improper. They hovered on the brink of something she knew was not the wisest to begin. He had no legitimate reason to be holding her hand, and she had no legitimate reason to let him. But the possibilities beckoning were too powerful to fight.

She took slow, lazy steps like his in the fashion she'd expect lovers might take to prolong the moment. The pounding of her heart drowned out the sound of their footsteps on the crushed stone. Two minutes. She'd only been with Lance two minutes, and she felt giddy. She closed her eyes. *Stapleton, you've created one helluva problem.*

His hand released hers. A tonal double beep made her realize she stood next to a gray SUV, an American-made model not as ostentatious as she imagined a politician's car might be. He opened the passenger door, and she slid inside. She watched him jog to the driver's side and get in. "Not the ride I thought you'd have."

He pressed the start button and the car roared to life.

"What did you expect?" He rested a forearm on the center console, looked over his right shoulder, and backed out of the parking space.

"A limo with American flags flying from the front grill and a driver, or maybe an Uber, but definitely not you behind the wheel of a soccer mom's car."

He laughed. "I like driving when I can." He pulled out onto the main road and headed away from Princeton.

Kate settled in. "Where are we going?"

"Lawrenceville. I know a deli on Division Street that makes a great Rueben."

"How do you know? Don't you spend most of your time in Washington?"

He clicked on the left blinker and turned. "I have a town house in D.C. I use when the Senate is in session and for official business in Washington, but I actually live in Lawrenceville. In the house in which I was raised, to be exact."

"Interesting." She mentally calculated it would take under twenty minutes to get from her home to his, which made the situation suddenly more appealing.

Lance cocked an eyebrow. "How so?"

"I never gave much thought to the secret life of politicians." Until now, she silently added.

"We all have secrets, Kate."

Unexpectedly, her heart slammed against her chest wall and turned on her reporter switches, compelling her to dig deeper. "What kind of secrets?"

"The kind someone accumulates over the course of his or her life. Why do you ask?"

She didn't know how to answer. She didn't like lying but saw no other way. "No real reason. We seem to kiss a lot but don't talk much about our pasts. I could read your official bio, but I don't think any skeletons you have in your closet would be listed there."

A half smile played around his lips. "Nope, but I do like the kissing."

She grinned. "That part isn't half bad."

He wrinkled his forehead. "Not exactly a testimonial to my technique."

"I won't give one without a bit more research." She winked. "Just to be sure." He smiled at her, his teeth white and even, and she let out a gratifying sigh. She really liked this guy.

A few minutes later, he pulled into a parking slot in front of a storefront deli and turned off the engine.

She shook her head and dropped her chin. "This is weird."

"What is?"

One side of his mouth quirked in a grin. "You pretending to need help with lunch, and me pretending to fall for that ploy when actually all we both really want is to spend private time together."

"I should have realized you would see right through me," he said.

Fighting the distraction of his dimpled, boyish smirk, she crossed her arms and shot him a challenging glance. "So, you've done something like this before."

"Once or twice, but nothing came of it. But since I met you at the reunion, I'm finding more reasons to hone the technique."

"Really?" She started to say more but noticed a flush along his cheekbones that wasn't there a minute ago. Something qualifying was about to come. "But?" She slowly released a breath.

"Politics, Kate. Affairs of state can be deadly to a new relationship. I don't spend a whole lot of time in New Jersey. I have two district offices, one in Morristown and one in Cherry Hill, with staff to handle any arising issues. I might be a senator with only six years on the Hill, but I know the game. Too much time away from D.C. has an impact on one's career." Lance hesitated, his eyes half closed. "You and I might be GUP's."

Kate blinked. "GUP's?"

"Geographically Undesirable People. Though I can commute back and forth on the Acela Express and get from New York to Washington in three hours, my free time is short."

She stared out the side window and mentally weighed the pros and cons. Before she looked back felt more like hours instead of seconds. "You're saying there's no room for us to explore any kind of relationship."

His eyes narrowed. "I'm saying I think we both need to do some clearheaded thinking."

Forcing the reporter switch inside her head to off, she lifted her eyebrows. "Can we at least date while we think?" His lips kinked into a smile that caused her pulse rate to speed up. The unexpected warmth now in his eyes melted away any defenses she still had against his charm. "Or maybe text once in a while."

His brows drew down. "I've already proven I can't think straight with you around. Putting something in a text message that can be recovered could be political suicide."

Everything inside Kate went cold, the enthusiasm she felt seconds ago instantly extinguished like water on fire. She mulled over Lance's comment and the truth attached. The two of them together did not make sense, but she could not let go.

Cursing her indecisiveness, a trait of which she had never been accused, she made a decision she hoped she would not regret. "I don't want to stop seeing you just because you think you have to give up a private life when you keep the world safe for democracy, and I can't handle all the strings attached."

He reached for her then pulled back. "I'm not saying we won't see each other."

"Then let's date."

He shook his head. "And let the political media dig into you with both hands? Remember what I said about secrets? Even if you have none, some reporter will place a seed of doubt inside a story, and suddenly, you're tainted for life."

Her mind flew to the worst-case scenario. "Is that what happened to your last relationship?"

"Not exactly. My being elected to the Senate happened."

"She hated politics?"

"She liked the image of being on a politician's arm.

She felt powerful and sexy. In fact, I believe my title was the main reason she flirted in the first place."

"I probably would have flirted, too." Kate saw an incredulous stare form on his face.

"You would?"

She nodded. "Theoretically, but only to talk to you, not get my picture in the Lifestyle section of the *Washington Post*."

His eyebrows arched. "You don't seem to be the type to read society news."

The voice inside Kate's head shouted a warning. Her mouth was about to get her butt in trouble. Time to tap dance. She forced a laugh. "My BFF loves to read Page Six in any newspaper." She put a hand to her chest. "Me? I'd rather read the sports section." She winked. "Giants fan."

"Another side of you I didn't know." He grinned. "But I can see a problem."

Her forehead wrinkled.

Lance jerked a thumb toward his chest. "Eagles."

Kate formed her mouth into a perfect 'O'. "You can always convert." Lance's ensuing smile brought alive his delicious dimples, and the happy gleam in his eyes would have been visible from space.

"Too bad we didn't meet before I won my first election," he said. "We would have had time to straighten out this football thing."

"Maybe so." The thought of the upcoming election reminded Kate of the small amount of time they did have left. An odd sense of loss overcame her. "I suppose the timing isn't right. When you win re-election, you'll be running off to that townhouse in D.C., but we can still be friends."

His lips parted. "I have friends, Kate."

"You don't need another one?"

"I don't want you to just be my friend." He held her gaze. "What do you think, Kate? Can we make something work?"

No missing the emotion behind the words. She swallowed hard and avoided his gaze. He held her chin and looked into her eyes until she could feel the heat in her toes.

"Maybe you need more than a friend, too."

His low, sexy voice caressed her and brought her senses alive. Why was she hesitating and disagreeing to discover what she could have with a man like Lance? Simple. She was the predator, and he was the prey. She wanted to smack him for making her feel things she didn't want to think about, especially on this assignment.

He ran a forefinger across her lips. "I want someone to keep me warm on those cold D.C. nights and to tell whatever is on my mind and not be judged but just loved." A long moment of silence passed before he spoke again. "It would be nice."

His fingers stroked her cheek, and she could not look away, even if she tried. Warmth flooded her. "Tell me what to do."

His chuckle diffused the tension. "I'm not sure anyone could tell you what to do. Your grit is something I like most."

She sighed. "Sometimes I feel conflicted. I like the way you make me feel, and a part of me wants more from this relationship, but my job—"

Lance laughed aloud. "I fail to understand why selling bathroom ads will ruin our relationship."

Looking away, she teetered on the verge of telling the truth, but his rich laugh and great smile stopped her. Shaking her head, she looked back. "My job is here, and your life is in Washington. One thing I know for sure, neither of us is ready to begin a new career choice."

Kate saw a myriad of emotion run across Lance's face. He said nothing to rebut her statement, only stared out the windshield. She raised a hand to brush his cheek.

But Lance caught her wrist midair. "If anything is meant to be between us, we'll work it out. Washington has taught me tolerance."

He relaxed his hold, and Kate slipped free of his grasp. "I'm not known for my patience, and stars aren't aligning to start anything lasting."

He angled in the seat and narrowed his eyes. "We could be about to miss the only chance we might ever get."

Honest. There was that word again. She wanted to confess, but the rueful note in his voice nearly broke her heart. She couldn't break his. She had to give him a way out. "I'm not a summer romance kind of girl, and you're—"

He raised a hand and pulled in a ragged breath. "And suddenly I'm a hit-and-run kind of guy?"

Guilt sank its claws deep. She should tell him the truth but feared anything she said would sound like the it's-not-you-it's-me cop out. Dragging a hand through her hair, she looked away. "Before I met you, I'd driven any thought of a relationship to the back of my mind. I had other things to do first."

"And now?"

She looked at him and shook her head. "Maybe we don't know each other well enough to risk everything we have now." Lance stared, as though trying to decipher what she wasn't saying. "Please understand. I want to grab onto this small chance with both hands, but I can't."

"Or won't."

Kate shrugged and looked down at her lap.

Lance shifted and grabbed the steering wheel with both hands. "Then this is just another lunch run."

Though she led him in the break-up direction, his calm accepting attitude suddenly irked her, proving she was not ready to let him go. She opened the car door so he could not drive off. "No! Forget lunch. Forget the campaign. You want to talk about us, so let's talk."

His eyebrows shot up. "Are we about to have our first real fight?"

"Probably." She slashed a hand through the air. "You started this convo, and you'll finish it before this car moves another inch."

Lance rested his back against the car door and held her gaze. "You don't understand, Kate. Election politics get really nasty. I don't know what is ahead. I can only warn you about what might happen."

She angled herself in the seat. She wasn't about to let him think she was a pushover. "What if I don't care about what people say?" That excuse sounds ridiculous. If she did her job correctly, she *was* the person who would say something awful. She lifted her chin another notch and hoped he couldn't see it tremble.

He let out a long breath. "As much as I want to be wrong about the timing, the campaign is taking every free second I have. Talking now will not make much difference when you start feeling abandoned because I'm on the campaign trail all hours of the day and night. I'm the one in politics, Kate. I don't have the right to drag you along until you know more about the darker side and can protect yourself."

She tilted her chin in a defiant gesture. "I don't need protection."

He stiff-armed the steering wheel. "You have no idea what Washington can do to a nice girl like you."

The analogy drained all fight from her body. She didn't feel like a nice girl, and she shouldn't be pushing something that probably would not have a good outcome. But her head was not in the same place as her heart. The wistful yearnings when she was with Lance were all too real, and something she had not encountered in years. She struggled with the choice between career and love. To explore a relationship, she would have to forsake her assignment and stand at Lance's side. But if she was totally honest with herself, she wasn't.

She tapped her palms on her thighs. "I give up. I can't argue the pros and cons of beltway duplicities, so I'll settle for lunch. But I warn you, this discussion isn't over."

Lance arched a dark eyebrow. "Truce?"

"For now." Kate pointed toward the deli. "BLT, extra mayo, chips, salad, and an iced tea."

"Yes, ma'am." Lance saluted and exited the car. A second later, he opened the car and ducked his head inside. "Want to come in?"

She shook her head. "I'm okay here."

He nodded and headed inside the shop.

Kate needed time to think, but her brain had gone

numb. Embarrassment wove its threads through her confusion. She should know what she was doing, but she had no idea. She pulled down the visor and stared into the mirror. As lifeless eyes stared back, she realized she might never be okay again. She was a fraud, and no amount of apologies would make anything right once the truth came out. "End this," she commanded the woman looking back "Rip off the tape and let him go."

The trouble was, once she broke her own heart in the process, she was sure she'd never be whole again.

****

Silence dominated the ride back to campaign headquarters. Lance glanced at Kate but said nothing. She sat low in the seat, one knee up against the glove compartment, her head turned slightly as she stared out the window. She gave up too easily. That surprised him. Were they over before they were even together? He hoped not.

A gust of wind through the lowered passenger side window caught her hair and whipped a strand across her lips. She blew out a short breath of air then brushed aside the lock. Another burst of air blew the curl right back. She spit out the strand and lopped it behind her ear.

He could not help but chuckle.

Kate turned and smiled. "Not very ladylike, huh?"

He grinned. "Maybe not, but kind of sexy."

She pointed forward. "Eyes on the road, Senator, or you might not have to worry about a re-election bid."

He nodded, and she resumed looking out the passenger window. Neither spoke again as he drove on.

Out of the corner of his eye, he could see Kate

mouthing the words to the song on the radio, and a smile grew as he suddenly recognized something great. He could comfortably share silence with Kate. Other women he dated acted as though quiet was an enemy and filled the void with frivolous chatter, but Kate was content just enjoying the moment. He wanted the chance to share more quiet moments with her, but timing and the odds were against him. He would take what he could now and hope for more later.

All too soon, the panorama of the back door of campaign headquarters filled the front windshield. "We're here," Lance announced.

Kate looked at him and frowned. 'Seems so."

Lance killed the ignition and hooked a wrist over the steering wheel. "Thanks."

"For what? Riding shotgun?"

The question was so benign it made him laugh. "No, for putting up with me and my politics."

Kate tossed her head. "I could say the same for dealing with me and my quirks."

"We all have those." He let out a long, slow breath. "I've been so involved with the re-election I've forgotten how to handle the rest of life."

She waved off the comment. "Life doesn't come with a teleprompter or a staff to help us through the awkward spots." She looked into his eyes. "I yelled at you, you yelled at me, and we settled nothing."

He laughed. "Sounds like a voting session on the Hill."

She looked long and hard at him. "Forget politics for a moment. What now?"

Was she asking about them? His thoughts froze for a second. "Now, we feed the masses before I have a revolt on my hands."

"Then?" she whispered.

She *was* asking about them. He didn't know what to say to allow her to make the choice, so he went with the obvious. "I have to get back to D.C. The voting session is rescheduled for Monday afternoon. I need to leave tonight and review some bills in the morning."

Kate broke eye contact. "Oh."

Save this, his mind ordered. "Can I call you some time during the week?"

Smiling, she nodded.

"I'll be back in New Jersey by the weekend." He looked toward the office. "Will you be here?"

She nodded again.

I sound like a geeky teenager asking the cool girl for a date. He gripped the wheel with both hands and stared at his knuckles. "I have a fundraiser next Saturday." He turned his head and caught her gaze. "I'd like you to go with me."

Eyes wide, Kate leaned back. "Like on a date?"

A sinking feeling settled in his stomach. He just asked her out, and she looked as though someone punched her in the gut.

She shook her head. "Not my thing. You should probably go alone. Won't you be spending most of the time shaking hands and convincing the attendees to add a few more zeros to their donation check to your re-election fund?"

"The Tin Man fundraiser is not political. The event is to help Joey and all those like him. People attending care less about my politics and more about finding a cure."

"But wouldn't lending your name to the cause also

bring more attention to your politics?"

He shook his head. "As I mentioned before, Joey has what is called an orphan disease. Not enough people are affected to get federal attention or funding. It is up to the families to raise money for research to find a cure or a drug to slow the disease's progression."

She frowned. "That stinks."

"More than you know." Holding tight to his hope, he stared at his hands for a moment. "So, will you join me?"

****

The hopeful look on his face convinced her. Kate touched his shoulder. "Anything for Joey."

He took her hand and twisted their fingers together. "Great, I'll call you midweek with the details." He started to get out of the car.

But she stopped him with a hand to his shoulder. "I need one detail now."

"Shoot," he said with a grin.

"What does one wear to a Tin Man fundraiser?" She anticipated a dress code and did not want to disappoint. "I'm a T-shirt and jeans kind of girl."

"Sorry. This one is black tie."

Suddenly feeling out of her league, she sighed. "Guess I'll have to get a gown."

"Need some help?"

She rolled her eyes. "You're kidding, right?"

"I am." He gave a weak laugh. "I don't know what I would have done if you accepted the offer."

"I can handle this." She touched his cheek in a brief caress. "You'll just have to trust me, Senator."

His answer was a weak, resigned rumble. "Since I got into politics, I'm not much good at trust." His lips curved into a smile. "But now seems like as good a time as any to start."

Kate winced and closed her eyes, feeling as if she were treading water in a pool filled with dark, murky liquid with no way to know the depth. He shouldn't trust her. Her job was to ruin him. She cast a quick look in his direction and then out the front window.

"Something wrong, Kate?"

She didn't immediately answer.

"Is it the fundraiser or me?"

She turned and smiled. "I just don't want to screw up. I don't know a salad fork from a dessert fork." She glanced down. "And then there's all the food that could miss my mouth and end up—" She pointed to her lap. "—there."

He laughed. "I know a pretty good dry cleaner."

The words 'but do you know a priest with a comfortable confessional, because I'm a fraud' weighed heavily on her tongue, but she didn't have the courage to give them a voice. Even as she called herself a thousand awful names, she had to move forward with her assignment. She could remember too many other times she wanted a chance to break the big story and get out of tabloid journalism but failed to get the task. Finally, after a few years of struggling, she'd been handed a chance. But success could only come at the expense of someone who could actually make a difference. The penance much, but after the dust settled, she'd write a story about the terrible disease he championed and maybe help. She'd still be an awful person, but maybe she could sleep a little better at night.

She sighed. "The drinks are getting hot, and the

food is getting cold. I don't want your volunteers getting food poisoning because I can't figure out what type of shoes won't give me blisters." She opened the car door and climbed out. "Let's go. I'll wear sneakers."

Chapter Eight

Over the rest of the weekend, Kate found writing about Lance easier when he wasn't with her. By Monday, she eked out two stories—one with a some creative license raising questions about Lance's social life, and the other bordering on great fiction concerning his views on climate change. But neither was the story Gartman really wanted. He wouldn't wait too much longer for copy asking what else Lance did in the campaign bus.

She logged out of the Internet search engine and closed her laptop. When she looked up, she saw Gartman standing at the opening to her cubicle. "Need something?"

Gartman crossed his arms over his chest and huffed. "A *real* story."

Kate almost laughed out loud. "Since when did *The Analytical* go legit?"

He scowled. "You know what I mean." He pulled a sheet of paper from his back pocket and tossed it onto her desk. "Subscriptions are up but not by much. I need your copy on the campaign bus topic ASAP, Kate." He placed both hands on her desk and leaned forward. "Unless you can't handle the assignment."

Conflicting thoughts raced through her mind. Something bad was coming next. Not wanting to get into a spitting contest, she did not take the bait.

"Or you don't want to." Gartman straightened. "Which is it? I know you've been getting cozy with the senator."

Kate ran a hand through her hair. "I'm on a fact-finding mission."

"Susan said otherwise."

Knowing Susan was on the other side and probably listening, she raised her voice. "I sincerely doubt she'd tell you anything."

"Relax, Stapleton. You're right. Your BFF didn't betray you. Not exactly, anyway. I overheard her talking on the phone." He smirked. "She does talk rather loudly."

Susan's head appeared over the top of the partition separating her work station from Kate's. "You eavesdropped?" She glared at him then looked at Kate. "I'm sorry. I had no idea the jerk skulked around after hours."

Gartman laughed. "Good reporters always skulk." He pointed at Kate. "You should try lurking sometime. Might improve your writing." He glanced at Susan. "You, too."

Susan rolled her eyes and disappeared behind the divider.

"I'll get your story." Kate clenched her teeth so hard her jaw ached. "But you can't run the copy until next Monday."

"Reason?"

"Timing." She didn't feel like saying anything more.

"Agreed. But this might be your last chance. I haven't decided if you're finishing the assignment."

She glared, wishing she possessed the same power

135

as Medusa. Gartman would look great in the park as a stone statue with a couple of pigeons on his head. "Oh, I *am* finishing this assignment."

"Then get a story that goes mainstream." Gartman pointed to the laptop and left.

Once Gartman's office door slammed, Susan walked into Kate's cubicle. "I am so sorry."

Kate raised both hands. "Don't apologize. I should have realized something would get back to Gartman sooner or later." The warmth of embarrassment crept across her cheeks. "I must have been distracted."

Susan snickered. "I'd say so. What's next?"

Kate tapped the desk top with her fingers in a staccato rhythm. "File the story, and be done with it."

"What 'it' are you talking about? The story or the senator?"

Kate saw the challenge in Susan's eyes. "The story."

"Don't think so."

Susan's sing-song voice made Kate grit her teeth to avoid commenting. She leaned her elbows on the desktop. "I really don't want to talk about the senator right now." She saw Susan flinch and was immediately sorry for her tone of voice. "Want to make things up to me?"

"Any way I can."

"I need to borrow a gown. The blue one. And the little black bag you used for the Correspondent's Dinner last year. The shoes, too. You do still have everything, right?"

Susan nodded slowly.

She saw about a hundred questions rise in Susan's eyes. "Don't ask. Just get everything to me ASAP."

****

In the back seat of the sedan he used for official business in Washington, Lance tapped the face of his smart watch and frowned. "It's still only Tuesday." He lay his head onto the headrest. "I swear the weeks drag on here in D.C."

"Only seems like it, sir." Jack eased the car into the garage of Lance's townhouse.

The sound of the door closing echoed in the small space.

He glanced in the rearview mirror. "Those stories in the niche news—" He shook his head. "No. That online rag isn't worthy to be associated with news. The trash story about you could win first prize in a fiction-writing contest."

"It's the silly season, Jack. I should expect to be attacked by my opponent and the media." He disliked campaign season. Most candidates seemed to lose their minds until after the election, but he vowed a long time ago not to resort to spite politics.

Jack angled his body toward the back of the car. "I can understand questions about your politics but not your personal life. Anyone who knows you would disagree about the posting and the allegation you use the campaign and the publicity to keep your rock-star persona intact and your social media followers interested."

Jack's voice sounded not only defensive but also extremely pissed. Lance sighed. "I don't want nor have a rock star persona." He could almost feel his blood pressure rise. "But I can't control the media, Jack. If my opponent wanted controversy, you can't argue with success. My poll numbers are down, and the negative comments are up on my media page."

"Not enough to lose an election."

"Not yet."

"You worried?"

An intuitive feeling something wasn't quite right crept along Lance's nerves. "Could be a concern."

"You should issue a statement deriding the articles."

Lance waved off Jack's suggestion. "Saying I'm a closet womanizer might be a low blow, but I don't want to give credence to any of what was written." He rubbed his brow with the thumb and forefinger of this right hand. "The media will be onto something else in a day or two."

Jack's forehead contracted. "Maybe not this time."

Lance forced some laughter and exited the back seat. Then he opened the door and heard the distinct clank of something hitting the garage floor.

Jack walked back to investigate and found Lance on one knee, palms on the ground, peering underneath the car. "What fell off?"

"Something shiny." Lance stood and dusted off his pants with a few swipes of his right palm. He tossed a strip of metal to Jack. "That whatever-you're-holding is why I like old cars. They have character, and they're built to last."

"The car's not old. Probably still under warranty. I'll have the garage pick it up in the morning." Jack looked at the small hunk of metal in his hand. "Guess this one's character was a little fast and loose."

Lance tilted his head and narrowed his eyes. "Are you referring to the car or to me?"

"Definitely not you," Jack said. "And if the so-called journalist took some time to research the story, he or she would find your character is a lot like an old car." He nodded. "Steady and reliable."

Lance laughed. "Thought you meant worn and cranky."

"Not in the least, sir." Jack tapped his palm with the car part. "I'll get the car to the dealer in the morning. Maybe the repairs will be a quick fix."

"How many years have you lived in Washington?" With hands on hips, Lance waited for the answer.

"About twenty."

"And you still don't realize nothing is ever a quick fix here? Every person and every entity on the beltway slow-walks everything." Lance snickered. "D.C. apparently exists in an alternate time continuum."

Jack joined in the laughter. "But just like the '69 Mets, sometimes you just gotta believe." He saluted his goodbye.

After locking the garage, Lance walked up the three steps and into the kitchen. He yanked open the refrigerator and grabbed a beer from the bottom shelf. He popped the top, took a healthy swig, and tossed his jacket onto the center island. After draining the beer in a couple gulps, he chucked the can into the sink and turned off the lights.

As he headed upstairs to the master bedroom, he stopped in the middle of the grand staircase and looked at the large foyer. He shook his head. Four bedrooms, five-and-a-half baths, thirty-five hundred square feet. The place was way too big for one person.

At thirty-eight, he thought he'd be married and well on his way to his third child, but his career led him down a different path. An overwhelming feeling of loneliness grew, and he suddenly needed to speak to Kate. He missed her. Right about now, he would do anything to hear her voice and get away from the D.C. toxic vibe for a few minutes. He did want to give her the details of the upcoming fundraiser. The excuse was as good as any to call.

His heartbeat rose as he dialed. After no answer in five rings, he figured he'd have to leave a message and rehearsed a few sentences about the same time he heard her voice.

"Hello?"

She sounded sleepy, as though the phone call pulled her from that moment between being awake and asleep. Visions of Kate with her hair spread out on a pillow flashed through his mind. A strange sensation of being flooded by warmth confirmed his suspicions. She had some type of hold on him, whether he was with her or not. "It's Lance. Did I wake you?" He thought he heard her yawn.

"No. I just turned off the TV."

He chuckled. "Was I on?"

She joined in the laughter. "Of course."

"Don't ruin the moment by telling me what the piece was about."

She blew out a quick burst of air. "Wouldn't think of it."

"I know it's late, but I wanted to give you a heads-up about the fundraiser." He slid the phone between his left shoulder and his ear as he walked to his bedroom unbuttoning his shirt. He palmed on the light switch. "The event starts out formal but if tradition holds, half way through tuxedo jackets and ties come off and so do most of the ladies' high-heeled shoes."

She laughed. "Internet search didn't cover those details."

"You checked on me?" He was glad she couldn't see his slanted grin.

"No, I checked on the event and learned more about the disease." Her voice dropped. "Awful circumstances."

"Sure are." Lance wandered the room as he spoke. "I also want you to know the keynote speaker canceled, and the organizer wants me to fill in. I told him yes."

"I wouldn't have expected anything less."

He weighed the pros and cons of what he would tell her next. "Now that I'm the face of this event, less time will be available for us. I'll have to do a lot of hand shaking, talking to donors, and posing for meet-and-greet photos. So, here's the deal. Since this event isn't looking like a first date after all, I'm offering you this one-time pass to back out. We can reschedule something else."

"After I got the perfect dress and matching handbag? Not on your life."

"Great!" He hoped he hadn't yelled his response, because inside the adrenaline flowed like a wide open water tap, and his stomach did the happy dance. "Cocktails start at six p.m., and I plan to arrive around six thirty." He heard soft laugher.

"We're making a grand entrance?"

"No, I'd just rather spend the first thirty minutes of the date talking to you."

"I'm flattered."

He heard the appreciation in her voice and wished he could see her smile.

"Jack coming?" she asked.

"No. He's staying in D.C."

"Ah, helping to keep the world safe for democracy while you're out of town."

"Nothing so exciting. Something fell off the car and he's getting it fixed."

"Anything serious?"

"I don't think so." He heard Kate yawn again. "It's late. How about I let you get some sleep before you get back to the wonderful world of marketing." The following silence seemed to last a lifetime. "You still there?"

"Yes," she said quickly. "About the marketing thing." She paused. "That's not what I do."

She sounded sad, but he didn't want to pry. "You'll find something better. Are you okay?"

"I am."

"I could make a few calls."

"No," she snapped. "I'll be fine. But I do need to get some rest. See you on Saturday."

When the call disconnected, Lance sensed she was holding something back. He brushed it off as his imagination and smiled. Maybe he wouldn't be alone tonight after all. Maybe his dreams would all be of Kate.

****

For a few minutes Kate stared at the phone, reminding herself the relationship, if that's what she could call what she and Lance had, was a temporary one. If he won the election, he would be knee deep sticking to his convictions in a pool of political barracuda waiting to smell a little blood in the congressional water. And if he lost? She had no idea what ex-senators did.

However, if Lance did lose his seat, the defeat would be partly her fault. No matter what she felt for him now, the guilt would outweigh the satisfaction of any media credit she might receive. One thing was certain. In victory or defeat, she would have to confess her deception. She did slip in a small morsel of the truth when she told him she didn't sell Johnny ads. Well, sort of told him. Clearly, he thought she either quit or lost the job, and she was too much of a coward to take the conversation any further.

Her head hurt. Her stomach heaved. She closed her eyes and took a deep breath. The queasiness she felt was not because she didn't come clean to Lance, but because the copy Gartman wanted was in his email.

She plugged her cell into the charger before dropping onto the foot of her bed and falling back. She stared at the ceiling. For the first time, she fully understood why the college professors in every journalism course she took warned about the pitfalls of getting too involved with the subjects of investigative journalism. Until the darn reunion, she was sure she could handle her assignment with detachment, but she was way past getting involved now. She was pretty sure she was falling in love with Lance. He was honest to a fault, genuine, funny and a hundred other adjectives, not to mention maddeningly attractive.

She rolled to her side and curled into a ball, struggling with the obvious. Between the invitation she accepted from Lance and the deadline she set with Gartman, she had one week to decide what to do.

Destroy Lance's career or hers.

Break his heart or hers.

Or possibly all the above.

Chapter Nine

Kate looked at the reflection in the full-length mirror mounted on the back of her bedroom door. She barely recognized the person who looked back. With a little help from Susan, Kate's brown hair swept up and away from her face under the control of a fancy hair clip. Because of the long looping curls Susan set with a fancy hair tool, her hair looked as though she added some highlights. She liked the style but knew tonight would be the first and last time her hair looked this good. She would never spend the amount of time Susan took to create the finished product. She was more a headband and ponytail girl.

On impulse, she pulled out her cell phone and snapped a selfie. She looked at the picture on the camera scroll. After Susan left, she toned down the eye shadow and amount of liner applied. Her eyes still looked great but now looked a lot more natural and a lot less like Cleopatra.

What she really liked was the dress. The blue color reminded her of the ocean. Not the ocean off the Jersey Shore, but more like an ocean in a travel ad for a great island vacation place. The A-line princess silhouette flattered her curves and the neckline dropped into a V-neck style just low enough to show a little cleavage. The asymmetrical hemline brushed the middle of her knees in the front and dusted the back of her calves in the back. The cap sleeves were lightly beaded in the same color blue, a touch she suspected would catch the light and make the trimmings sparkle. Dangle earrings, a simple silver chain around her neck holding the small diamond locket she received from her grandmother, and a bangle bracelet on her left wrist, and she was good to go.

This is crazy. She was about to go out on an official first date with the most eligible politician in the country, and she was not even registered to vote. What would Lance think once he saw her? The daydream made her heart flutter. When she placed a hand on her chest, she realized she was sweating. She was more into this date than she imagined.

She heard a car pulled into the driveway, and she looked out her bedroom window. Her brow winkled. It wasn't a car, but it was Lance. She zeroed in on him like a wild bird finding its mate within a flock of a hundred. He glanced in her direction, but she was sure he couldn't see her.

After slamming the door, he strolled toward her front door.

Kate flew down the stairs and stopped short of the foyer. Tempted to yank open the front door before the doorbell rang, she called on every bit of restraint and waited. The sound of the bell hit her like a bolt of lightning. After taking a deep breath, she pulled open the door, and something warm exploded within her heart.

Lance's smile was more brilliant than she remembered. When his gaze swept over her from head to toe, a weightless sense of expectation flooded her.

He extended his hands. "You look absolutely

beautiful." She put her hands in his, and he leaned forward and kissed her cheek.

The warmth spreading up her chest meant she blushed. "You don't look so bad yourself." A bit of an awkward pause followed. "Do you want to come in?"

"Sure." He followed her inside.

"Sit anyplace you'd like." She circled the center island separating the living room from the dining area. "Can I get you something to drink? Trying to talk Susan out of making me look like a fashion model made me thirsty."

He smiled. "You look great."

Kate pointed toward her face. "This is the after. I did some adjusting after Susan left."

"Whatever the adjustments were, they worked."

"Don't get used to all this face paint. It isn't me." She arched a brow. "But I did take a selfie just in case." She headed for the kitchen. "Sure I can't get you something?"

"I'm fine," Lance called after her. "Take your time."

She peeked around the open refrigerator door. "I'll be right in."

****

As he walked into the living room, Lance heard ice clinking into a glass. He chose a side chair by the fireplace lit with flickering flameless candles creating an impression of warmth and romance. For a fleeting moment, he wondered if Kate fashioned the ambiance for him, or was the idea simply his wishful thinking. The tug to find out was hard to fight.

Kate emerged from the kitchen and sat on the sofa across from him. She slid the glass of ice water onto the coffee table. "How much time do we have before we need to leave?"

He angled his watch toward his eyes. "Maybe a few minutes." He looked around. "Nice place."

"Thanks. I was thinking of selling about three years ago, so I tore down a few walls to open the space and make the house more sellable."

"You were thinking about moving out of New Jersey?"

She nodded. "I wanted to explore other opportunities but changed my mind at the last minute."

Lance leaned forward and rested his forearms on his knees. He laced his fingers together. "Well, I am glad you stayed. If you moved, we might have never met. Right now, you might even be working to get my rival elected."

"Oh, I doubt it." Kate shook her head and smiled.

He raised a forefinger. "Ah, I remember. You did say you disliked politics."

She mimicked the gesture. "But I am warming to the thought."

****

Whatever she expected when she saw Lance on her doorstep, the response was not to be so captivated by a man in a tuxedo. Never again would she consider black a boring color after seeing it stretched across Lance's fabulously toned body. Snowy white splashes of crisp fabric streaked around his neck and wrists in stark contrast to the dark fabric defining his shoulders and arms. The distinction was tempting, inviting her to engage in forbidden exploration of what might be hidden underneath.

"You seem a little nervous." He straightened.

"Something wrong?"

Her breath released in a rush of air. "I guess I am. You must go to dozens of black tie events every year, but this one is my first."

His eyes widened a bit. "That surprises me."

"Why?"

He hesitated. "Because if I could, I would take you to every state dinner in Washington."

Unaccustomed to compliments, Kate smoothed the hem of her dress. "I suspect after one or two minutes, I'd say the wrong thing to the wrong person and end up creating some sort of scandal by morning."

He laughed. "Would be interesting. Washington society can be a bit stiff." His smile crinkled the corners of his eyes. "Bet you'd given them a run for their money." He stood and held out a hand. "What do you say we see how it goes tonight before you rule out a second date?"

She took the hand offered and rose. "I can't promise I won't use the wrong fork or not drop crumbs all over the linen tablecloth."

"I'm not asking for promises," he said. "I want you to be yourself." At her front door, he stopped. "But I have a slight problem."

A sinking feeling settled in Kate's stomach. "What? My dress?" She looked at her feet. "The wrong shoes?"

He laughed. "The mode of transportation." He pulled open the front door. "I drove Jack's pickup. My car is still out of commission. Jack stayed at the townhouse in Washington, so he could get the car from the shop early on Monday. I didn't want to waste time finding a rental. Hope you don't mind."

Kate shook her head. "Not at all." Her heart skipped a few beats. "Sounds like you plan to stay in New Jersey for a few days."

"I'm hoping to have a reason to do just that."

Kate read the twinkle lighting his eyes as anticipation. "Let's see how I do at this fancy dinner. You might want to get out of Dodge fast."

He displayed a wide grin. "You'll be just fine. The people attending are not politicos. They are the everyday salt of the earth folks who just want to help."

"Then I have a chance."

He waited until she locked the door and then took her hand.

She didn't even pull away as they walked down the steps and to his truck. She looked from the passenger side door to Lance and then back at the truck. "In these shoes and this dress, I'm not getting in there like a proper lady." She swore she saw him smirk.

He opened the door. "The best I can do is offer you a hand." He extended his palm. "Either that, or we can call a cab."

Kate hiked her dress to mid-thigh. "No need. I can do this." She turned and grinned. "But no fair helping me inside with a hand to my backside."

Lance's mouth fell open, and he dropped his hand.

Laughter rose from Kate's throat. "Relax, Mr. Senator. I got this." She put one foot on the rail and one hand on the seat and with a jump propelled herself up and inside. She smoothed her dress and buckled the seatbelt. "Now let's roll before you're late for your own speech."

Grinning the whole time, he circled to the driver's side and slid inside. "You are something else, Kate

Taylor." He started the truck.

Kate almost choked on the truth in his words. She was something else...someone else to be exact. He'd know soon enough. But for now, for tonight, she'd be Kate Taylor. Former Johnny ad saleswoman and current date of one of the most eligible bachelors in Washington, D.C. She buried the chagrin deep inside her gut. "Yes, I am." She raised her chin. "And if I am not mistaken, tonight so are you something else."

His quizzical look made her smile.

"Tonight, you are not a high-powered legislator, but you are an activist for a very worthy cause."

He nodded and backed out her driveway. "Sounds like a plan." He turned right, heading toward the main drag, a wide, four-lane commercial street leading to the interstate.

"Where is this shindig?" Kate asked.

Lance put on the blinker and merged into a line of cars. "Shindig. Now that's a word I haven't used in a long time."

"Let me rephrase then." She cleared her throat. "At what hour do the festivities begin?"

He shook his head. "Still not Washington-speak."

"Translate then."

Lance squared his shoulders. "Our entrance will be approximately thirty minutes into the cocktail party. We are to proceed to the benefactors' area and mingle appropriately."

Kate grimaced. "Sounds stuffy."

"Will be until after speeches. Once the honorees and benefactors leave..."

"You mean the mucky-mucks."

His smile flashed. "Yes, once the mucky-mucks

leave the shindig"—he winked—"the band starts playing, and the atmosphere morphs to the second part of the evening."

"But aren't you one of the mucky-mucks?"

He shrugged.

Kate formed her mouth into a perfect 'O' and raised her eyebrows. "You've never stayed for part two, have you?"

"Not exactly."

"Well, this time you will." Her voice rose excitedly. "You said a band will be there, and I like to dance."

Lance turned his head for a moment and looked at Kate. "I'm looking forward to it, Kate. I think tonight is just what I need."

Maybe the hint of laughter in his voice made her feel giddy, or maybe the Cinderella feeling growing inside made her reach out and touch his cheek. Whatever happened, Kate felt free of the façade she created for herself as they spent the next half hour driving and getting to know each other better. During that precious time, she was herself.

They talked about family, traded funny stories, and discussed her future and his life after politics. The sense of familiarity and building fascination spun a web of undeniable attraction. Laughter came easily, and flirtation was inevitable.

Kate turned to glimpse his profile with renewed interest. "I wish we would have met sooner," she said. "We did go to college in the same town." But years apart, she silently added. She waited eagerly for his comment, hoping to get an idea about whether he was as interested in her as she was in him.

He studied her silently, and then turned back to scan the road ahead. "I don't know if you would have liked me back then. I was a bit of a rebel."

"How so?" A flush of adrenaline tingled through her body. Was this her lead story for the next edition of *the Analytical*? As quickly as the thought came, she sent her reporter instincts packing. She wanted to enjoy the evening and enjoy Lance. Tonight could very well be the last opportunity she might have.

He laughed. "Long hair, big mouth. I protested when the mood struck me and a lot of times just because a pretty girl asked me. I earned a reputation as a campus rabble-rouser and got caught up in a sit-in sweep." The light at the intersection turned red and the truck rolled to a slow stop. He looked at her and hesitated for a moment. "We thought we'd be charged with trespassing, but charges were never filed."

The startling revelation sent a shiver up Kate's arms. Imagine what she could do with a lead like that. Gathering every ounce of morality she could find, she refused to allow herself to be tempted to ask for more details. "I think we all did something back in the day we wish we hadn't."

"So, what's yours?" Lance asked.

"I have a few." The car behind honked, and she realized the light turned. She pointed. "Light's green."

Lance acknowledged the impatient driver behind with a quick wave and drove ahead. "So, what are your regrets?"

"Once I dyed my hair bright green."

"You'll have to do better."

She tapped a forefinger across her lips and thought for a minute. "I do have a tattoo. A tramp-stamp on my lower back, but you can't see it."

"Not yet." He displayed a wide grin. "Anything else?"

"When I was in high school, I sprayed graffiti on my neighbor's new fence, got caught, and endured a station house adjustment lecture when the neighbor didn't press charges." She rolled her eyes. "I apologized and offered to clean the fence, but the compromise wasn't good enough for my dad. He made me do twenty hours of community service *and* clean the fence."

Lance chuckled. "You win." He suddenly pulled onto a rest area off the interstate.

Not a full-service stop, this one was a small strip with a few picnic tables, some large trash cans, and vending machines in a three-sided structure. The only other car pulled out shortly after Lance turned off the engine.

Then silence surrounded them. "Is something wrong with the truck?"

"No, but I've wanted to do something since you opened your front door." He slid as close as the center console allowed and slipped one hand behind her head. Gently, he pulled her closer.

Kate did not resist. In a slow, smooth movement, she leaned toward him and placed a hand on his chest, signaling her consent.

Lance kissed her with a soft exploratory pressure packed with self-control.

His lips were warm and parted only slightly. The kiss lasted only about ten seconds but for the last five, she gripped his lapel and drew him closer. Just before he broke the kiss, his lips parted, and he swept his tongue across the seam of her mouth. Her lips dropped open just as he retreated, too late to encourage the kiss to become more intimate or to last longer.

She looked into his dark eyes and felt his heart thudding against the palm of her hand. She didn't pull away but could not think of one coherent thing to say.

Lance stroked the hollow beneath her lower lip with his thumb.

The slightly rough feel of each caress on her skin brought her heightened awareness. "I wanted to kiss you too."

Lance's eyes sparkled, and he brushed a lock of hair from her face before he straightened. "I might take you up on that after the fundraiser is over."

"And I might let you," Kate said.

He put the car in gear and headed out on the interstate.

As soon as the words were out, Kate's reporter side resurfaced with a terse warning. *What are you doing? You shouldn't be encouraging something that will blow up in your face and break your heart as soon as the truth gets out.*

This time, she didn't send away her alter ego but hoped the pieces of her heart once broken would somehow knit back together with none of the parts lost so she would feel whole again.

Chapter Ten

A beautiful country club in northern New Jersey hosted the benefit. A perfectly manicured golf course surrounded the majestic brick clubhouse that resembled a stately mansion. A few cars had already pulled up to the stunning architectural eye-catcher. As Lance's pickup inched forward in the valet parking line, Kate saw the jacketed attendants frown.

"I think they are worried about tips," Lance teased. "Among an array of luxury cars, this model doesn't exactly scream 'here's a twenty'."

As the truck stopped, Kate laughed. "Wait until they see who gets out." She reached for the door, but Lance stopped her with a hand to her arm.

He climbed out and started around the front of the truck but stopped when a few attendants recognized him and called out. He acknowledged each valet with a handshake.

She suspected he shared polite small talk because the simple act of handing over the keys took about ten minutes.

Finally he reached the passenger door, opened it, and extended his hand.

As she took it, she savored the contact. She gestured with her chin toward the valets. "A preview of what is to come?"

"Afraid so." He dropped her hand and turned her

by the elbow toward the door. "I promise to speed up the process if I can."

"And I promise to adapt." She winked. "If I can."

The organizer and his staff greeted Lance and Kate as soon as they reached the huge glass entrance doors. "Senator, glad you could help us by stepping in as keynote."

Lance acknowledged him with a nod. "Please call me Lance." His head turned toward Kate. "This is Kate Taylor. She was gracious enough not to let me come alone. Kate, this is John Adams. He's the nerve center of this benefit. He's a passionate advocate for those who have this rare disease and the thrust behind making sure they aren't forgotten."

John held out a hand, palm up.

Kate cupped her hands around his. "Lance has been telling me about this event. I very much wanted to attend with him."

John gestured to an area to the right just inside the door. "If you'll both follow me, a few of the patrons are waiting to meet you before the event officially begins."

With Lance's hand at the small of her back, Kate stepped inside and took notice of the setting. The cocktail hour was well under way, and she estimated a few hundred people milled around. Some with drinks in their hands engaged in grouped conversations while others accepted appetizers set on silver trays from servers. A large group of patrons waited in lines in front of one of five bars set around the anteroom. The doors to the banquet hall were still closed, each guarded by a formally dressed attendant. "Yikes," she whispered. "This is more ceremonial than I suspected."

He dipped his head. "You're doing fine, and I

really appreciate it."

"I also suspect you'll owe me big time by the time the night is over."

"I think so," Lance replied.

John pushed open a side door and led Lance and Kate into a room filled with fifty or so patrons and their guests.

Almost immediately, the crowd closed around Lance.

Kate would have to wait until he could break free. Out of the corner of her eye, she saw a woman approach.

"I'm Addy," the woman said.

Kate nodded. "Kate." She drew down her brows. Who was this person? "Are you one of the organizers?"

The woman quietly laughed. "I see Lance hasn't filled you in completely."

"Apparently not." By using Lance's first name instead of his formal title, Kate knew the woman was obviously a bit more than an event coordinator.

Addy glanced toward the throng. "John will save Lance in a few minutes. In the meantime, can I get you something to drink while we wait?"

"Seltzer would be great." Kate followed Addy to a small table and sat at one of the two chairs. She waited until the waiter took the drink order. "Are you part of the fundraiser?"

"I've done events with Lance about four years now. And you?"

"I'm afraid I'm not as savvy. I just learned about the illness last week."

"I'm not talking about the ailment." Addy slid her elbow onto the table and leaned closer. "How long have you been seeing Lance?"

Kate lifted her brows. Her thoughts raced as she tried to decipher why Addy probed her personal life within minutes of meeting. Was she an ex not ready to let go? "I'm not seeing him. We're just friends."

"Are you now?" She held Kate's gaze.

Annoyed, Kate decided to stop the interrogation with a one-word answer. "Yes."

Addy glanced at Lance who acknowledged her by lifting his chin. "He's very handsome, isn't he?"

The server set their drinks on the table top.

"If you like the GQ type."

"You don't?"

"Those tall, dark, and perfect types aren't for me." Was it her imagination or did Addy perk up a bit with the denial?

"So, you wouldn't mind if I stole him for a dance later?" Addy picked up her drink and scrutinized Kate over the rim as she sipped. "I mean since you aren't a couple or anything."

"Dance away." Kate did not like this woman. "Lance is free to do what he wants with whomever he wants, so I have no idea why you are investigating a relationship that does not exist."

Addy sat back. "You don't mince words, which makes me think your interest in Lance might go beyond friendship." She smirked. "Does it?"

Kate donned her best fake smile. "To answer your most inappropriate question, especially since I've already defined that Lance and I are just friends. If you want to dance with him, or anything else for that matter, knock yourself out." *Literally.* She didn't wait for a returning comment but simply plucked her water from the table, stood, and walked away. She found an empty chair near the coat check to wait for Lance to finish with the formalities.

****

About fifteen minutes later, Lance found Kate. "I've been looking for you. What are doing here in the hallway?" The angry clenching of her mouth and flushing of red on her skin told him something was wrong. "You look...troubled. Is everything all right?"

Kate crossed her arms. "I ran into a friend of yours."

His brow furrowed. "Can you narrow it down a little more?"

She stood. "Small dress, big hair, blonde, and not natural, I can assure you."

He saw her eyes darken. "You must mean Addy."

"Good friend of yours?"

"Just a friend. Over the years, she's been my plus-one at a number of benefits here in New Jersey when Maxie was busy."

"You dated her?"

"I wouldn't call meeting at an event and then leaving in separate cars much of a date, so no." He narrowed his eyes. "Why do you ask?"

"I was about to be grilled on whether or not I was in a relationship with you before I shut down the conversation."

Rather than ask the obvious question of how she responded, Lance chose another approach. "I'm sorry. Sometimes supporters get a bit possessive."

"Possessive, you say?" She huffed. "She marked her territory."

Lance grinned. "Want to tell me what happened?"

Kate folded her arms across her chest. "No."

His grin turned into a laugh. "Do I detect a slight bit of jealousy in your tone?"

"How do you get jealousy from a simple, one-syllable answer?"

"We politicians learn to read body language rather quickly."

She pointed to herself. "Then my body language should be telling you I am not the least bit jealous." Was she sending out green vibes?

He tried not to laugh but failed. "Of course."

Kate was about to respond but glanced over Lance's shoulder.

"Senator, the guests are being seated." John gestured toward the filling room. "Shall we?"

Lance placed a hand on Kate's elbow, leaning close. "I promise I'll make it up to you if you just bear with me and tough out this evening."

Kate looked away for a moment and watched the cocktail area thin of guests. "I'm sure things will only get better from here." She looked back. "What's next?"

They followed John toward the head table, and Lance acknowledged some supporters with nods and a raised hand. "The event gets formal for a little while. Dinner is broken by speeches and a short clip on the disease and the devastating effect it has on the patient and the family. Next, the Head of Research at University Hospital will update us about the progress made in the past year. Then, when dessert comes out, people start to leave. Once that happens, the band sets up, and the rest of the night is kind of ad lib and, I promise, a lot more fun."

****

Inside, mostly everyone was seated now. Kate noticed very few empty chairs in addition to those at the long head table in the front of the room. "Do we just find our places at the head table?"

Lance shook his head. "I suspect we all will be introduced in a few minutes and seated in the proper pecking order. Doctors first, then the researchers, then us, and lastly, the family being honored tonight."

Kate had no time to ask more questions.

John walked to a podium positioned to the left of a large screen and began the formal announcements. Each introduction garnered rousing applause.

As the introduction of Lance loomed she suddenly felt a little more uncomfortable. "Shouldn't I wait in the hall until all the introductions are made? I would rather not call attention to myself." The hum of reverb coming from the PA system told her no time remained for an answer.

"And we all know Senator Lance Michaels." Applause rose.

Lance grabbed her hand. "When we get to our places at the table, don't sit just yet," he whispered. "Follow my lead."

She nodded and didn't try to pull her hand free. He was the pro, and she was the novice. She only hoped she wouldn't do something to embarrass him like trip over a chair leg or fall off the back of the riser on which the head table rested.

The acknowledgement from the attendees, complete with whistles and friendly shouts continued. The standing ovation he received was louder and more robust than any introduction before his. Kate dipped her head and tried to make herself as small as possible so she could hide behind Lance, but the long, single-file path to their places felt like a walk down the red carpet. Though Lance raised his right hand to indicate his appreciation of the accolades being offered, his other firmly held hers.

When all the honored guests were introduced, Lance stepped behind her chair and held it until she sat before moving to his seat.

Kate rested an elbow on the table and set her chin on her knuckles. "She is staring," she said, through clenched teeth once he sat.

"Who? Addy?"

Kate smiled to hide her annoyance. "Uh-ha."

Lance leaned toward her. "She'll get over it."

Kate turned up the wattage on her smile. "Not likely because I intend to give her something to think about." She pressed her cheek to his and dropped her voice to a hush. "What color is she now?"

Lance glanced in Addy's direction. "Bright red."

"Any smoke coming out of her ears?"

"Can't tell. A server is in the way."

Seeing the server approach, Kate moved away from Lance.

"Champagne?" the man asked.

Kate lifted her glass. Her little game was sidetracked, but she was certain she made her point. The moment of satisfaction was very brief until she noticed a myriad of flashes coming from cameras.

Now all she could think about were the social media sites putting up a picture of her and Lance holding hands or huddled close in a corner in what could be misconstrued as a very intimate moment before dinner. She hoped her image would be cropped out of the picture, but she guessed that probably would not happen. Celebrities, rock stars, and yes, even politicians had their groupies, too, and groupies always wanted to know about the "plus one". She already met uber-groupie Addy. No doubt more attended the event. Social media would explode once Addy logged into the site and posted. But no sense stressing. She had no control over what Addy might say, so whether she liked it or not, this event was her coming out party. She'd have to handle the fallout later.

When John began his welcome speech, the clink of glasses and low buzz of conversations immediately halted. After a few minutes of cursory thank-yous, the benefit speeches began.

"Our first speaker needs no introduction, but I'll do it anyway," he said.

A twitter of laughter rose from the crowd.

"Senator Lance Michaels has been a patron of this cause long before being elected to office. I believe I got involved when he met our special honoree, Joey Heywood, and his family at a small fundraiser in Union, New Jersey, a few years ago." He glanced at Lance. "About eight years, right?"

Lance nodded.

A spotlight then turned on and settled on Joey who sat at the far end of the head table with his mother and father.

John waited until the applause faded before continuing. "We all know Joey has something special that grabs your heart and doesn't let go."

"I'll say he does," a woman seated at an end table shouted.

Joey smiled and turned red.

His mother leaned over and kissed his cheek.

"See what I mean," John said.

Nods and a low hum of agreeing voices slowly faded.

"Ever since Senator Michaels met the Heywood family, his commitment to them and those affected by this terrible illness has helped bring awareness to the cause." He gestured toward the head table. "I am thrilled to announce that due to the dedicated work of Senator Michaels, I received word this morning from Washington the National Institute of Health has promised to take a hard look at getting some funding for research."

The room suddenly exploded in applause and whistles.

John gestured for quiet. "Senator Michaels didn't know I would be announcing that bit of good news, and I'll probably catch hell. So before he throws a dinner roll or fork at me, I'll let him do his thing." He extended a hand. "Ladies and gentlemen, I give you Senator Lance Michaels."

The patrons applauded as Lance made his way to the podium.

Kate could not take her eyes off him. He had the easy manner of someone totally relaxed and sure of his place in the universe. He shook a few hands on the way to speak but didn't linger long enough with any one person to slow the pace of the evening. She knew he had probably delivered the speech like the one he was about to give hundreds of times at a myriad of events, yet his mannerism did not contradict the impression this one was the most important one of all.

As she watched and listened, she could not help but

wonder if the time she spent with him was thought of the same.

****

Lance returned to his seat. "Sorry I had to abandon you, but duty called. I hope you weren't too bored."

"No apology necessary. After that speech, I bet there are plenty of high-powered executives who will be loosening the grip on their wallets. I know I want to."

His engaging grin twinkled.

Kate clutched his hand. "You really hit home with what you said."

"Thanks. Every little bit counts until I can convince Congress to permanently loosen the purse strings to fund more research for this illness in the national budget." He turned his head and glanced at Joey. "These kids…" He stopped.

Did she imagine it, or did his voice break a little?

"These kids have to deal with an insurmountable challenge, and it breaks my heart. We do our best to help with their quality of life, but even though we do what we can, it feels like we hit a brick wall." His thumb made slow circles on the back of her hand. "And that wall isn't coming down any time soon." He looked into her eyes.

Kate could see sadness overtake the glint his eyes held just a moment ago. His emotional sincerity tugged at her heart, throwing her into career limbo. Trapped by the choices she made so far, she almost confessed but stopped. This wasn't the time nor the place. This event was much more important than her. "We should probably pay attention to the rest of the speakers," she said softly.

He drew down his eyebrows. "Is everything all right?"

She nodded. "Just digesting that emotional speech." The look of accomplishment in his eyes made her breath catch. She gestured to the next speaker. "Bet he won't get anywhere close."

Later, when the formalities were finally over, some of the attendees said their goodbyes and headed for the door. Others, energized when the four-piece band took the stage and began the first set, started dancing.

Even Lance's somber mood changed. He captured Kate's hand and led her toward the dance floor. Once there, he swooped her into his arms. "I'm not exactly Fred Astaire, but for better or worse, we dance!" He tightened his hold, rested his jaw on her temple, and settled her hips into his.

With the contact, Kate felt an immediate rush. With Lance this close, the faint scent of his lime and cedar cologne filled her nostrils. She wasn't accustomed to smelling a man's neck, but at the moment, she liked the idea a lot.

As they danced, she felt the scrape of an emerging beard where his chin met her temple. She moved her hand from his shoulder to the back of his neck and rested her forefinger just above his collar. Controlling the temptation to move her hand higher and tangle her fingers in his hair, she moved her hand back to his shoulder, content for the moment to take in all the textures and scents she experienced as she danced in his arms.

"What are you thinking?" he whispered against her cheek.

"The program was long, but I could feel the

sincerity in each of the speeches." Kate matched her movements to his and swayed in time to a second slow song.

Lance backed away slightly and looked into her eyes. "I didn't mean the formalities." He winked. "But I confess we are a bit longwinded when it comes to this cause."

Kate laughed. "Can't say I've ever met a politician who wasn't."

"Really? And just how many have you met?"

His voice shaded with amusement. "Counting you?"

He nodded.

"One."

Lance pulled her closer and continued to dance. His hand moved caressingly on her back. "Then I don't have much competition." With her in his arms, he made two dramatic turns before laughing into her ear as he lost his balance on the second and stepped on her foot. He grimaced. "I told you I'm not Fred Astaire."

"I don't need Fred Astaire," Kate said. "You'll do just fine."

The next few songs were fast ones, and Kate was pleasantly surprised when Lance stayed on the dance floor. He rocked his shoulders and moved his hips in time to the beat. Every now and then, a woman would dance up beside him and join in, but he always made sure he returned to finish the song with her.

"You aren't half bad at this," she quipped.

"So I'm half good?"

Kate lifted her chin and laughed. "Half good then."

"I'll take it."

After the upbeat set finished, Lance removed his

jacket and draped it across the back of the nearest chair. A slow song started, and he extended his hands. "I'm not ready to quit just yet."

Kate moved back into his arms. She let her fingertips explore his shoulder blades and the hollow between them. In response, his arm tightened around her waist. She sighed and nestled into his hard curves while he dropped his head until his lips rested just beside her right ear.

'Whatever perfume you are wearing smells great," he whispered.

His lips brushed her skin with every word. "Glad you approve." Her chest rose and fell against his, causing heat to rise on her neck.

"Does it taste as good as it smells?"

A chuckle rumbled from her throat. "I don't know. Does yours?"

His fingers moved to her ribs. "Maybe we can both find out later."

"Maybe, maybe not," she murmured against his neck. "Depends on how the rest of the evening goes."

"Then I better make sure it goes well."

The next set consisted of four fast dances in a row. They danced until their brows were damp and their breaths short. Kate fanned her face with a hand. "Good aerobics. I might have worked off the dessert."

Lance took off his tie and stuffed it into his pants pocket. "Keep moving. I ate about three dinner rolls." He rolled his sleeves to the elbows. "This dancing is hotter than a debate with those across the aisle in Washington."

Kate huffed out a laugh. "Want to go outside for a minute and cool off?"

He grinned and nodded. "Sounds like a good idea. Let me grab my jacket, and you grab your purse in case we want to ditch this place," he added.

As they crossed the dance floor on the way toward the back of the banquet room, Lance shook hands with friends and supporters. Just before they reached the door, one man stepped out and blocked their way.

He pulled a check from his inside coat pocket. "For your re-election campaign."

Lance looked at the amount. "While I appreciate the gesture, I'd rather you donated to the fundraiser." He held out the donation. "This amount could do a lot of good. Maybe buy a piece of needed equipment." He fixed his gaze on the supporter's face. "What do you say we make that happen?"

The man looked at the check in Lance's outstretched hand for a moment before taking the check. "I'd say yes." He ripped the check in half.

Lance grasped his hand and shook it firmly. "I really appreciate your generosity." He smiled. "And I do hope you have another check with you."

A grin formed on the supporter's face. "I don't, but I assure you I will mail one tomorrow, because I know you'll call if by some chance I did forget. Then, somehow, you'd talk me into doubling the amount."

Lance laughed. "You can still do that."

The supporter patted Lance on the back and walked away.

Kate cocked her head and stepped outside the banquet room. "Do you hear that?"

Lance drew down his brows. "I hear the music and a low din of voices. Is that what you mean?"

She grinned. "No, but for a moment there, I

thought I heard angels singing." She took a small step back. "You are the real deal, aren't you?"

Lance shook his head. "The only real deal I know is the one that takes us out of here." He grabbed her hand and headed for the exit.

The hand-holding didn't last long as they ran into a group of benefactors in the parking lot. After a few more minutes of Q and A, some selfies, and a chorus of 'good night, Senator', Lance walked to the pickup and unlocked the doors. He stood silent for a while at the door of the passenger side, looked up, and scanned the star-draped sky.

Kate followed his lead. "Something interesting up there?"

He checked his watch. "In about an hour there will be." He saw her eyebrows furrow. "Meteor shower."

"Really?"

"I check the Farmer's Almanac every year and try to catch at least one."

She leaned away. "Is NASA one of your committee assignments?"

He grinned. "I wish. Since I was a kid I've been fascinated by the stars. Matter of fact, I wanted to be an astronaut until the tenth grade, and I took my first airplane ride at a local airport." He shook his head. "Got sick as a dog. Still do."

Kate cut her gaze to his. "You're kidding."

"As serious as a heart attack. Jack makes sure I have plenty of barf bags when we fly."

"Modern medicine has a pill for that, you know."

He narrowed his lips and shook his head. "I hate taking drugs for anything. I've see too many lives ruined through addiction."

****

Kate bit her lip, though she would have rather bit her tongue. "Oh. Forgot. On a lighter note, I must admit, I have never seen a meteor shower."

"Then you are in for a treat, if you're game." He opened the passenger door. "But this is no place to watch it. Too many city lights here."

Kate slid inside and settled in the seat. "What do you have in mind?"

"In order to really see the stars and the meteors, we have to get to a field or a place away from the ambient light." He winked. "Trust me?"

"Hmm." She tapped a forefinger on her chin. "Trust a politician. Sounds like a trap." A sly grin grew. "But I'll take a chance."

"Good." He closed the door and sprinted to the driver's side. Once inside he buckled his seat belt and started the truck.

Kate slanted toward him and stared.

"What?"

She shook her head.

"Change your mind?"

"No. I just never imagined someone in politics would be so…conventional."

"Conventional?" He smiled. "I've been called a lot of things, but never conventional."

Her breath caught. She looked at the curve of his lips and remembered how wonderful they felt on hers.

Now, Kate, don't get any ideas about kissing him. If you do, you'll set the tone for the rest of the evening and be in for one helluva problem.

Somehow, she tore away her gaze and looked out the windshield. She leaned forward and looked up at the stars. "If you make me miss my first meteor shower, I might call you a few other things. Let's move."

Chapter Eleven

Lance pulled onto a dirt road that cut into a field about ten miles outside Princeton. About another mile later, he brought the pickup to a stop next to a crumbling barn.

"I distinctly saw a No Trespassing sign on the fence before we turned," Kate said. "You're breaking the law, Senator."

A touch of humor laced her voice. "Not exactly." Lance turned off the ignition. "The place belongs to my cousin. I've helped the family by milking a cow or two in my youth. I doubt he'll press charges." He got out, walked around the front of the truck, and opened her door. Then he held out a hand.

Kate stashed her bag under the seat and held onto his hand as she eased out of the car. "You are full of surprises. Who would ever think the sophisticated legislator would be a farm boy at heart?"

"As I said, we all have secrets." He made sure she settled firmly on the slightly uneven ground before he slammed the door. He led her to the rear of the pickup. There, he let down the tail gate and gestured to the truck bed "No other place to sit but here." He glanced at the abandoned field. "Or the ground."

Kate toed the dirt and then patted the tailgate. "I suppose I could hop up here if you give me a hand."

"I have a better idea."

Before she would have the chance to ask him what he had in mind, Lance picked her up and settled her against his body.

She laughed and circled his neck with her arms. The laughing abruptly stopped when she looked into his eyes.

When their gazes locked, he heard her inhale sharply then hold her breath. Her mouth was close enough to see each tiny line in her lips. The urge to kiss her flooded him like a breaking levee, but he knew the risks if he acted on the impulse.

"Maybe you should slide me onto the tailgate," she whispered.

He hesitated Though he did like the way her body felt against his, the sense of the forbidden surrounded him. What was he thinking wanting to be alone with her? For a moment he'd forgotten how predatory the media could be if they were discovered. He had no right to drag her into that lion's den. But he just could not let her go.

Hs wrenched his mind away from the imagined media circus and stared into Kate's eyes. His mouth felt suddenly parched. "Maybe this isn't such a good idea after all."

****

Lance's tone sounded suddenly dull and lifeless. She narrowed her gaze and searched his features. "What changed over the last ten seconds?" She looked at the sky. "Meteor shower suddenly canceled?"

Gently, Lance set her on the rear hatch and hopped up next to her. He clasped his hands and rested his forearms on his thighs. He looked at her but said nothing.

"What are you thinking?" Kate saw him rub the back of his neck and knew something else was on his mind.

"In your opinion, would it be wrong for a man who is totally wrapped up in his career and the consequences of decisions he makes to ask a woman to accept second place for a while along with all the innuendo and media hounding sure to come and wait while he chased a dream?"

A slow exhale tempered the slight upward tilt of his lips. Kate tried to interpret the emotion in his eyes but saw only two deep shadows from which he studied her. She dared not think how she would answer him. "Probably a million reasons exist why that would not be a very good idea." However, something inside her wanted him to ask. "But the woman in question might think the result could be worth the effort, so the man in question should probably ask."

"Okay then, another question. Would that same man dishonor said woman by kissing her first knowing when he did, he might not be able to stop thereby delaying asking the first question in fear of getting the wrong answer?"

One side of her mouth quirked up in a teasing grin. With the playful back and forth, she sensed his guard was coming down. "Again, said woman possibly agreed with the resulting action of question number two, perhaps question number one could wait."

Lance laughed. "You sound like a seasoned politician."

Kate placed a hand on her chest and widened her eyes. "Lordy, I hope not." She swept her free hand in an arc. "Look around. Not a podium or microphone or reporter in sight." Lance's fingers tangled with hers and, his thumb made lazy circles on her skin.

"Thankfully."

Kate cupped his cheek and watched his mouth move closer. When their lips touched, she shuddered, and a shaft of fire ran through her. After a series of impassioned but quick kisses, she pulled back. "Do we know what we are doing?"

His fingers stroked her hairline just above her eyelids. "Probably not."

"Then maybe we should just watch the meteor shower." Her voice sounded throaty.

"Maybe." He did not move away.

She didn't either.

Lance's gaze roamed her face before it settled on her lips.

She knew what he wanted. She wanted the same. "Lance, you aren't playing fair."

"I'm not playing. Something special happened the night we met."

A shaft of guilt rose inside Kate as he leaned forward to kiss her again. She slanted back and covered his lips with her fingers. "You don't really know me. You could be making a huge mistake." Foolishly, the nebulous warning was as much as she was willing to give.

Lance took her hand and placed it on his chest over his thudding heart. "I know you're here for the same reason I am."

Kate dropped her chin and looked at her hand on his chest. Beneath her palm, she could feel his heart hammering like a jackhammer. She looked up. "Why do you think I came?" She saw him smile.

"To find out if more than just a casual friendship can happen between us."

Kate closed her eyes and took a deep breath. Fight your feelings, she told herself. Don't succumb to the guilt eating you alive. "Lance, I—"

"Don't plan anything right now. Just enjoy the moment." Lance released her hand and held her close. His warm mouth smothered the words she tried to say and drove everything from her mind.

Her head slanted and moved in slow circular nudges with gentle but exploratory and totally unhurried kisses. She pressed closer, and their kisses tangled as they learned other's textures from rough to smooth. The musky scent of his aftershave rose in a by-product of the heat generated. His cinnamon taste filled her mouth and, though the kisses remained gentle, she could also feel the restraint and swallowed the sound of rising emotion threatening to escape from her throat.

Lance lifted his head and smiled. "No turning back now, Kate. We're officially in a relationship."

Goose bumps prickled her skin, and she dropped her chin onto his collarbone. Her head felt weightless, but her body felt heavy as an attack of conscience punched her in the gut. Lance was a very good man. How could she continue to play a game in which he didn't even realize he was a pawn and not bring him disaster? She drew back, searching his face.

With a forefinger, he lifted her chin. "Kate, I want you in my life."

She cupped his cheek. "I can't deny I feel something for you, too."

Lance's lips thinned into a sharp line. "I sense a 'but' coming."

As she wondered how to tell him she would be his poison, Kate's heart thudded almost painfully in her chest. "Under normal circumstances—"

He ran a finger across her lips to stop her. "In my line of work, circumstances are never normal. I have no right to ask you to navigate the D.C. swamp as it is known these days, but I stay up nights thinking a relationship with you might work."

She hesitated. A sour tang filled her mouth. "What if you're wrong? You said it yourself. The time between the primary and the general election is the silly season." The ache beneath her breastbone deepened. What started as an assignment that could catapult her out of the tabloid business had turned into something so much more with an amazing incredible man whose life she could not bear to ruin. "I hate politics. Never watch the news unless it is to cover a natural disaster or check on the weather." She took his right hand in hers. "Maybe I'm just a temporary raft in the murky water, and just someone to help you forget the pull of lobbyists, filibusters, and mudslinging for a little while. Come November, we have to face reality. You're probably Beltway bound, and I will stay here, forgotten somewhere between fixing the opioid crisis and balancing the budget."

His hand rose in a defensive move. "Kate, you're wrong. We have something special. I can see it in your eyes." He looked at her mouth. "I feel it in your kiss."

She considered his words. He might very well be right. She'd never been affected by a man quite this suddenly and completely. She'd dated plenty of men in her twenty-eight years, and none before Lance raised her temperature this quickly or this fiercely. To think she considered throwing away her career to confess all to a man who could make sure she never worked in media again spoke volumes to how she really felt. Yet, she was not ready to take the chance of losing him by dragging him into her reality. Not yet. Immobilized by her indecision, she pressed her lips together.

Lance curled a strand of hair around her ear. "Was I wrong?"

She held his gaze. Why did his question sound as though he already talked about the past? "You do know bringing together opposite ends of a magnet repels and, worst case scenario, could cause a rip in the time-space continuum and tear a hole in the universe."

Lance smiled. "Then it is a good thing I voted to raise the defense budget."

Kate sighed. She was tired of fighting. Falling in love wasn't in her game plan, but it happened. She hadn't told him, maybe would never tell him. She should have resisted, but doing so was just too hard. Like Adam and Eve, they shared a bite of the forbidden fruit. The deed done, she could only hope to minimize the consequences. In a few weeks, Lance would be back in Washington, and she'd remain here. His job would take up most of his time, and she had no idea if she would even be employed. In the blink of an eye, her game plan had altered. She broke every rule and fell in love. The finish line was in sight, but the path forked, and she still had no idea if she would take the right or the left path. She gave Lance a tight-lipped smile. "One day at a time?"

"Agreed."

"I'll make some mistakes."

"I will, too."

"You're making one now." She pointed upward.

Lance looked up and saw a meteor streak across the night sky. "Right. The shower." He took off his jacket and folded it into a pillow-sized square. 'Scoot back. One never knows where and when a meteor will appear. I've always found it helpful to watch the show while lying down."

Kate tucked the jacket behind her head and lay onto the truck bed. Just as she looked up, another meteor raced across the sky. "Amazing. I don't know what took me so long to discover something this beautiful."

The truck rocked as Lance settled beside her. He eased close enough to touch her, but not enough to smother. He rose on an elbow and stroked her cheek. "Neither do I."

Kate laughed and looked upward. "Show's up there, Senator. There's nothing for you down here." She took a long slow breath to steady the excitement rushing though her body. *Yet.*

****

Lance had just dropped Kate at her house when his cell rang. Jack's number appeared on the dashboard display. As he turned onto the interstate and headed home, he answered via the Bluetooth connection "Checking on me?"

"No, sir, but I do need to talk to you."

Jack's voice sounded somber. "About something serious?"

"Could be."

"Is it the election?"

"Also, could be," Jack confirmed.

"Okay then, shoot."

180

"I'd rather not go into the details by phone. When will you be back?"

"Tomorrow. I'm leaving after breakfast." Lance's mind spun with possibilities, but he decided he couldn't do much about anything at 2 a.m. "On the brighter side, I just dropped off Kate at her place. Best date ever." The ensuing silence bothered him. "Jack, you still there?"

"I am."

"You're the one who keeps telling me to get out, find someone, and have some fun. I just told you I had the best date ever with an incredible, intelligent, and beautiful woman, and you have nothing to say?"

"Sir—" Hesitation laced Jack's voice.

Something was wrong, and Lance had no intention of waiting until the morning to find out. "Out with it, Jack. We can discuss the details when I get to Washington."

"It's about Kate."

Lance ran through various scenarios. She was married. She owed the IRS thousands of dollars. She was a Russian spy. He dismissed each as unreasonable except maybe for the IRS. "What about Kate?"

"She isn't the person you think she is."

Lance scrambled to figure out what Jack meant. "Of course, she is." He heard Jack take a deep breath.

"Sir, if I am right, what she might be could cost you the election."

For a moment, everything inside Lance went cold. Jack's serious tone and straightforward answer could only mean one thing. Kate had lied.

Chapter Twelve

At the office the next day, Kate stared at her laptop screen, career and honor warring inside her. She couldn't do what Gartman wanted. She couldn't destroy the career of a man who was probably the only politician in Washington who truly cared about his constituents. She logged onto the paper's server intent on deleting the story she sent to Gartman before she went to bed and was horrified to see the piece no longer in his inbox.

Inhaling deeply, she tried to calm her hammering heart. Gartman was probably editing the copy now. She couldn't let him put his version on the Internet. She started toward his office, but the roar of her name winding down the path between the cubicles made everything inside her go cold.

"Stapleton. In here. Now."

As she approached his door, she felt as though lead encased her feet. Once inside, she went on the offense. "I need to talk about my piece."

He kept typing without looking up. "Good, because that's why I called you in."

Positivity raced through Kate's mind. The copy wasn't yet live. When she saw him hit Enter, dread replaced optimism. "Please tell me you didn't just post my piece."

Gartman sat back. "Sure did, but with some edits."

Wariness rolled over her like a breaking wave. At times, Gartman's edits meant an entire rewrite. "How many is some?"

He gestured for her to sit.

She suspected whatever came out of his mouth next would not be a rave review and braced herself for the critique.

"Truthfully, the piece read like an eighth grade essay." He clasped his hands behind his head and leaned back. "White-bread boring to be exact."

Deep breath, Kate. She shot him a hard look. "What did you do?"

"I gave the copy to Benson. He fixed it, and I added a few finishing touches."

The white noise inside Kate's head that started as a buzz when Benson's name was mentioned grew to a mind-blowing roar when she imagined how the story would read after the tag-team fictional journalism. She opened her mouth, but nothing came out.

"Relax," Gartman said. "You still have the byline."

"I want to see that version." She hoped her voice didn't sound as horrified as she felt.

"It's live. No prob."

The anger building inside her overtook the panic rolling around her stomach. "Senator Michaels is a great guy. He might be the only sincere politician in Washington. He deserves to be re-elected. We can't put trash on the web that could jeopardize his career."

Gartman snickered. "Maybe you can't, but I can. No one wants to read about butterflies and rainbows." He shooed her away with a flicking wrist. "Be grateful you still have a job, considering the fluff you turned in."

If the heat on her cheeks was any indication of the look on her face, she knew Gartman could read her body language loud and clear. "Fluff? You arrogant jerk. I turned in a good story. An honest story." She stood, put both hands on his desk, and leaned forward. "I'm going to my cubicle now, and I intend to read the copy. You'd better hope I agree with the changes."

"And if you don't?"

Hesitating, she had no immediate answer. She didn't dare threaten to quit. Her job might be the only way she could generate damage control if the story going live was as condemning as she suspected. She glared for a long moment. "And if I don't, I'll write a retraction." A vein pulsed at her temple. "Better yet, an apology."

Gartman stood. "You wouldn't dare. This is my paper."

Kate straightened and made herself as tall as possible. "For now."

****

Two hours, forty-three minutes later, Lance was in Washington. Record time. The pick-up screeched to a stop in his driveway of his townhouse. He didn't wait for the garage door to fully open but ducked inside when it reached halfway. In two long strides, he was at the door and ripped it open.

Jack waited on the other side.

"What the devil do you mean Kate isn't the person I think she is, Jack?" Lance slowly and deliberately placed the knuckles of his clenched fists on the marble island top, leaned forward, and glared.

Instead of answering, Jack motioned for Lance to follow him into the study where two shot glasses of scotch waited. Jack picked up one and sat behind the antique desk.

The tension in the room hung in the air thicker than a pall of smoke. Lance reached for the remaining shot glass and glanced at the bottle from where it came. "My Macallan Rare Cask Black. Five hundred a bottle." He took a small sip. The amber liquid burned a path down his throat, allowing him a momentary distraction. He looked at Jack. "This must be serious." Unhurried, he pulled out a chair and sat across from Jack. "You have my attention."

"I told you on the phone Kate wasn't the person you thought she was." Jack gestured to a pile of paperwork in a wooden tray at the edge of the desk.

Clenching his jaw, Lance fought the urge to grab the top file folder. "Go on."

Fingers laced, Jack slid his wrists onto the desktop. "I had a feeling about her, so I did a little digging."

Lance's heart thudded inside his chest. "I asked you not to."

Jack nodded. "You did, but you are too trusting at times. I consider analysis of individuals part of my job."

"It isn't." Lance had no idea how he remained in control. He wanted to reach across the desk and shake the heck out of one of the finest men he knew for casting this shadow. He clenched his fist so hard his fingernails cut into his palm.

Jack nodded. "I know, but I checked her background anyway."

"Obviously." Lance pointed toward the folder.

Jack claimed the file and slid it across the desktop.

Something flared in Jack's eyes when Lance met

his gaze. He lifted his chin in acknowledgement. "What's in it?"

Jack sat back. "Read it. Then I'll either answer any questions you have, or I'll get my stuff and head for the unemployment office."

Lance held Jack's gaze as he covered the folder with his palm and slid it closer. The apologetic look in Jack's eyes could only mean no positive outcome.

****

Benson leaned against the frame of Kate's cubicle, arms crossed over his chest. "Like it?"

She cringed at his satisfied but totally arrogant smile but managed to read the revised copy. Slowly, she looked up from the computer screen. Cold fury clamped her heart, and the sound of his voice made her blood pound hard enough to start a headache. Not wanting to show the disgust the man provoked, she kept her gaze level with his. "Do you know what you've done?" Trying to maintain her composure, she spaced the words evenly.

Benson dropped into the chair opposite her desk. "Yes. I turned a piece of garbage into great copy." He hiked a thumb over his shoulder. "I just came from Gartman's office. Subscriptions to *the Analytical* are coming in fast and furious." He grinned. "Bet I get a raise."

Kate's stomach heaved. Striving to keep calm, she sucked in a gulp of air. "You worm." She held his gaze and parroted the headline. "Campaign Bus or Love Shack?" She spun around her laptop. "The only words in the story that are actually mine are the prepositions. None of your so-called editing is true."

"Relax." He dismissed her protest with a swipe of

his hand. "We're not here for God's-honest truth. We're here to entertain."

Benson looked condescendingly amused. Her anger climbed like a building hurricane. "Your rewrite insinuates Lance invited innocent women to his campaign bus and, once there, took advantage of the fact the RV is moving fifty-five miles per hour so they can't leave. God only knows what the readers will think."

He leaned forward and grinned. "I think God knows."

Kate pounded a fist on to desk top. "This story isn't a joke, you moron!" Her head spun, and she felt dizzy. She took a deep breath. "You've put a big black spot on his reputation without any evidence and suggest a well-hidden history of womanizing and possible hush money payoffs that I know do not exist."

Benson held up his forefinger. "Correction. You have the byline, so technically you've tainted his reputation."

Horror gripped her, and she felt all the blood drain from her face, He was right. The copy said *by K. A. Stapleton.* Bewildered about his lack of concern, she slumped back in her chair. "How could you?" Her voice sounded as helpless as she felt.

"Easy," Benson answered. "Mostly, I used the delete key on your copy."

His accompanying laughter only stoked the fire in her gut. She stood and pointed beyond him. "Get out," she ordered with a dramatic pause between words. She picked up her stapler and lifted it to her shoulder.

"Easy." Benson rose, his stare fixed on her hand. "I'm going."

As he stepped out of her cubicle, Kate heaved the stapler in his direction and missed his head by inches. It hit the edge of the frame and landed in the hall.

A hand waving a white tissue appeared at the edge of the door. "Don't shoot. It's Susan." She poked her head around the partition and waggled the stapler. "You could kill someone with this." She walked in and slid the makeshift weapon onto Kate's desk

"My idea exactly." Kate fell into her desk chair. "I can't do this, Susan."

"Sure you can. I'll swear Benson fell forward onto the fire extinguisher."

Kate flailed both hands in the air. "Though I'd be doing the world a favor, that's not what I meant." She slammed the laptop. "It's this job and this assignment. I can't let Lance get hurt."

Susan grimaced. "You saw the story."

"You mean the fairy tale fiction."

"I knew the writing wasn't your style. I came in early to stop any bloodshed." She glanced at the stapler. "Good thing your aim was off."

Kate stood. "I have to warn Lance." She grabbed her purse from the bottom desk drawer. Then she remembered he was in Washington. She dropped her shoulders and sat. "He went back to D.C. this morning."

"Then call him." Susan pointed toward the phone. "Don't let the circumstances gain any more traction."

"Confession isn't something I should do by phone."

Susan shook her head. "Unless you can teleport, I don't see a way to get to him quickly."

Kate pressed her lips together. "Then I'll call him."

She picked up the office phone.

But Susan took it from her hand. "Before you call, you need a plan."

"It's too late for that. I have to tell him everything," Kate replied.

Susan's eyes widened. "Everything?"

"Everything." Kate sighed. "The whole dirty truth."

"And then?"

"Ask for forgiveness."

"Good luck with that." Susan handed Kate the phone."I got your back." She stood and pointed to the right. "If you need me, I'll be right on the other side of the wall."

"No, stay. I need the moral support." Kate's heartbeat rose with every ring, but the call went to voice mail. "He isn't answering."

"Maybe that's a good sign. You'll have time to think."

"Thinking would've been nice a few weeks ago." She tried calling again. Voicemail.

"Think positive," Susan said.

Kate nodded. Nothing short of a miracle could save her. Like a ten-ton boulder, heaviness settled in her chest. Lance probably already had been briefed about the story from an aide assigned to check social media. She had no chance to get to him first. Anything beginning between them was almost certainly already gone.

****

When he closed the folder Jack handed him, Lance didn't look up. He slid his forearms onto the desk, clasped his hands, and stared at his tangled fingers. "K.

A. Stapleton." He looked at Jack. "She's been using me since the day we met at the reunion."

"Two glaring questions need immediate answers."

The heaviness in Jack's tone was unmistakable. Lance leaned back in the chair and gestured for Jack to continue.

"Who hired *The Analytical* to write those articles and why?"

"The opposition," Lance suggested. A muscle as tense as coiled steel moved along his jaw line. He was nowhere as calm as he tried to remain. What he felt was more than betrayal by an opponent or an insignificant online tabloid. He had fallen in love with a woman who played a role for what had to be merely some type of personal gain.

Numbness spread though his whole body. Since he was elected to Congress, he had been careful to avoid entanglements and serious relationships. Yet in the span of a few short weeks after meeting Kate Taylor, Johnny-ad saleswoman—correction, K. A. Stapleton, tabloid reporter—he lost his heart.

Disappointment welled, but disappointment in whom? In a woman who was apparently only doing her job, or in him for not realizing what could happen? He had to admit Kate was good. He'd fallen with the proverbial hook, line and sinker. He thought he was savvier than to get caught up in the Beltway power smokescreen of a beautiful woman choosing a mark and then feigning interest purely for the potential power wielded. Turned out, Kate was one really good actress. "What do we have, and how do we fix this?" The diamond hard edge to his voice camouflaged the pain he felt.

Jack straightened. "First, we have your girlfriend, Kate."

Lance held up a hand. "First, you need to separate her name from the word *girlfriend*." When he admitted to himself how much he wanted to be able to say otherwise, he curled his hands into fists. "I took her to a dinner, did some campaign stuff with her, and talked about a few more dates. Nothing more."

"Except take her for a spin in the campaign bus." Jack raised his eyebrows.

"Where nothing happened," Lance snapped. At least nothing they both didn't want, but he didn't want to admit the kiss to Jack. They had a campaign to save if they could.

"Doesn't matter," Jack replied. "The Internet is forever. Even if you sued *The Analytical* for defamation and distortion of the facts, retractions still get buried somewhere in the back. The original story will haunt your career forever."

"What else?" Lance asked. He fought to control his racing thoughts as he imagined a mud-slinging campaign ad taken out by his opponent.

Jack rifled through the papers. "We have to deal with your"—he glanced at Lance—"lady friend."

Before he answered, Lance paused. "I'm assuming you have a plan." He lifted his chin. "What do you have?"

Jack read the first page. "Kathryn Stapleton, twenty-eight, a graduate of Boston University where she majored in journalism. *The Analytical* is her first and only job in mass media since then."

"BU. Good school, good credentials for a career in writing, and yet, she works for an Internet scandal sheet." Lance wrinkled his brow. "Wonder why she doesn't have a legitimate job in the business."

Jack shrugged. "Maybe she likes destroying people's reputations. After all, she doesn't have to worry about sticking to the facts in her line of work. Look how well she made up her alter ego, Ms. Taylor."

Lance glared. "Forget about the fictional Kate Taylor for the moment." He wished he could. "Have my Chief of Staff put out a short counter story to set the record straight."

"Do you think that will be enough?"

"It's a start. I don't want to give any suggestion of real credibility to this trash, especially with the rash of recent accusations of inappropriate behavior by current celebrities and former politicians. Have the press room writers concentrate on my denial of everything and my affirmation I have the upmost respect for women and women's rights. Heavily underscore that neither I nor anyone associated with my campaign has ever been accused of any wrongdoing. End with a paragraph about how legal is looking into the story with an eye to a formal denouncement and a possible lawsuit."

"Right away, sir." Jack stood. "And what do you want me to do about Kate?"

"Nothing." He traded stares with Jack. "And I mean it this time."

Jack tightened his grip on the folder. "Yes, sir."

"You got one pass. You won't get another."

Jack nodded and left.

Lance sat silent, staring at the manila file folder breaking his heart. He opened the top right desk drawer, slid the file inside, and slammed the drawer shut before catching sight of the shredder on the floor next to the desk. He moved his gaze between the shredder and the drawer. *Get rid of it.* He shook off the thought. Shredding the paper wouldn't change anything. *You could pretend you never saw what was inside.* Ridiculous. Too many unanswered questions remained. *Then give her a chance to answer them.*

He leaned back in the chair, rested his elbows on the right armrest, and splayed his fingers across his forehead, a thumb resting on his cheek. He closed his eyes. Could he do what his heart suggested? Could the thin, single thread of hope his mind just spun be enough to listen to an explanation? He mulled over the answer for a very long time.

His happiest moments had been with Kate. She made him forget the game-playing, the back stabbing, and the deal-making of the career he chose. With her, he felt safe enough to look for meteors in the back of a truck and just be himself. He had to hear her explanation, no matter the outcome.

With the decision, a sudden realization struck him. What he felt for Kate was more than a passing fancy, and he could never just forget her and let her go.

Maybe he really was in love.

Chapter Thirteen

The next morning, Kate was the first one at the office. She had not slept. She slid an elbow onto the desk, rested her forehead on her palm, and listened to Lance's voicemail greeting. Despite leaving five messages, he still had not returned her call.

When the story broke, she called his cell every half hour and expected he'd answer. She planned to tell him everything, but with each voicemail she left, the dread building inside her grew larger. Somehow, he must know the truth. After the evening they shared, why else would he not answer her call?

The press release put out by his Public Information Office in response to her story was headline news. The statement was clipped, precise, and to the point in denying everything. She hoped his constituents believed more in his stellar reputation than in the trash with her byline on the Internet.

A knock on the partition wall preceded the voice. "Hey, you okay?"

Kate acknowledged Susan with a weak wave. "Sorry. I didn't know you were here."

"From the look on your face, I doubt you would have noticed a truck passing by."

Kate bit her bottom lip. The pain released some tension. "To answer your question, no, I am not okay." She gestured toward her phone. "I've been calling

Lance since last night. He's not taking my calls."

"Maybe he's busy with something on Capitol Hill."

Susan's clumsy attempt at a weak smile did nothing to relieve Kate's fears. She rubbed her temples with her fingertips. "What he's busy with is damage control."

"But he still should take your calls. He doesn't know you and K. A. Stapleton are one and the same."

Kate took a deep breath and closed her eyes. In her mind, she replayed what she knew and then looked at Susan. "I think he does." Her voice cracked. "He has all sorts of resources at his fingertips in Washington. No doubt someone, maybe Jack, did research on *The Analytical* once the story broke."

Susan's brow furrowed. "Who is Jack?"

"Lance's head of security. He is fiercely loyal, good at his job, and I can tell he is more than just an employee. I suspect after he read the article, he started some serious digging into *The Analytical* and K. A. Stapleton."

"But my nerd friend removed your picture. So even if Jack did some detective work, there isn't a trail directly to you."

"Oh no? All sorts of ways are available to recover any information on the internet. I'll just bet Jack knows some reformed hacker who can get him anything he needs just like Penelope Garcia does on *Criminal Minds*."

"Does this Jack look like the hunky guy who left the show? Because if he does, just like Penelope, I'd get him anything he needs, too."

Kate frowned. "Your attempt at lightening the situation isn't working."

Susan raised her shoulders. "I gave it a shot."

"I have to talk to Lance before this situation gets any worse." Kate reached for the phone.

"Won't he be at the campaign office in Princeton this weekend?" Susan asked.

"Maybe, but by then it will be too late for apologies and explanations." Despite the scald of beginning tears, Kate strengthened her resolve. "I have to do something now." Again, she punched in his number. "If I can't get him, I'll have to talk to him in person."

Susan slapped a hand to her waist. "Well, you can't drive all over D.C. stalking a senator."

With the back of her hand, Kate wiped a tear trailing down her cheek and left another voicemail message. "I can go to his district office and ask to see him."

"I suppose you could, but if what you fear is truth, he might have you escorted out before you get a chance to explain."

Kate bit her lip. "That's a chance I have to take." She grabbed her purse and started to walk out.

Susan put a hand on her arm. "Are you sure you want to do this?"

Kate bit her lip and looked into Susan's eyes. "No, but I don't have a whole lot of choices at the moment."

****

A knock preceded Lance's office door opening. His Chief of Staff took one step inside. "Senator, you have a committee meeting in twenty minutes, and Ms. Taylor is still waiting to see you."

Lance looked up from his laptop. "Thank you."

"She's been waiting for over two hours, sir."

He knew how long she'd been waiting. Lance let out the breath he'd been holding since he heard Kate's name. "Thank you," he said again. "Tell her I'll see her shortly."

The staffer nodded and left.

Lance started to sign some documents, but he could not concentrate on his signature. His rational side was so angry at Kate's betrayal he never wanted to speak to her again, but his heart needed an explanation that made sense. How could he have been so wrong?

He'd always been the cautious one and, since he took office, routinely used his career as an excuse to block every attempt at an emotional involvement. Eventually, he believed he could recognize anyone who had an ulterior motive. He grimaced. How incredibly stupid he'd been for not recognizing how isolated he had become. By focusing on the work he needed to do and his plans to save the world by righting every political wrong done by his predecessor, he had rationalized his loneliness. However, along the way, he apparently forgot to save himself.

He closed the laptop and pressed the intercom. "Send in Ms. Taylor, but tell her I only have ten minutes."

"Yes, sir," his Chief of Staff replied.

A moment later, the office door slowly opened, and Kate entered. "I know you're busy, but we need to talk."

When their gazes locked, Lance did not flinch. He stood, the gesture being more out of basic respect for a woman entering the room rather than being happy to see her. "I don't have much time." He gestured to the chair in front of his desk.

She leaned forward. "Then I'll talk fast."

He heard the quaver in her voice. "You have ten minutes." He folded his hands on the desk and braced himself for an onslaught of warring emotions. Didn't matter how much time he gave her because it already felt like ten hours since she walked through the door.

****

Kate barely heard Lance speak and didn't remember walking to the chair across from his desk. Suddenly, she was petrified. After she sat, she balled her hands into fists and rested them on her lap. Doubt rose. Maybe she shouldn't have come. Perhaps the time they spent together should be left as a pleasant memory. But she knew she couldn't. She might be scared, but she had been raised to admit her mistakes and face the consequences, and that's what she would do.

She took a deep breath and faced him. She could see the tension in his eyes and feel the icy bite of betrayal in the room. Her heart ached when she thought this could be the last time she saw him. "Thank you for seeing me."

Silence met her statement. A silence so cold she nearly shivered. Small infinitely deep doubts turned to quivers of pain in her stomach as she waited for Lance to say something.

He sat back. "I have a very important meeting in a few minutes..." He leveled his gaze. "...Ms. Stapleton. I don't think we have much to say to each other."

Heart pumping, Kate took a deep breath. He did know. "I owe you an explanation." The words did nothing to explain the lies she'd spoken over the last few weeks, nor the guilt she felt telling them. But she hoped her clear acceptance of the deception would be the start of an explanation he could accept.

"Perhaps apology would be a more fitting word." Lance opened the top right hand drawer and pulled out a folder. He slid it across the desk.

Her heart stopped as she picked up the file. She held his gaze but said nothing. A few tension-filled moments passed.

"You might want to open that."

Kate's mind nearly crumbled into darkness. She slid the folder back across the desk. "I don't have to read this. I know what's inside." Something flared in the depth of his eyes as he watched her, but she kept her gaze level.

"Good." He stood. "Then we have nothing to talk about."

She refused to stand and concede the meeting was over. "I think there is." Inside, she was crumbling, but outside she was steel. She tilted her head. "Give me a chance to explain."

Lance assessed her through narrowed eyes and sat. "If you can."

She took a deep breath. "Ever since I was a little girl, I wanted to be a reporter."

"We all have dreams, but most of them don't involve deception."

She barely heard him over her pounding heart. "Please. Let me finish."

He gestured for her to continue.

"I wanted a more legitimate job with mainstream media, but the only permanent job I could land was at a tabloid. I was a stringer for a local paper, and my resume wasn't exactly packed with anything of journalistic constancy. I had few options at the time.

What could I do?" She raised her voice for emphasis. "I had to pay the rent."

"At my expense," Lance added.

Kate shook her head. "Probably at mine. I've been working at *The Analytical* for three years, and that addition doesn't help my resume." She glanced at the file folder. "My assignments were all junk and then—" She stopped, suddenly not knowing how to express what had to be said. The depths of Lance's eyes were raw with turbulence. On top of dishonesty, she was about to heap hurt. "Then I received what I thought would be the assignment of a lifetime, my breakout story, and a chance to get out of the trash writing business. My boss wanted your secrets, and I told him I'd get them."

She expected him to lash out or at least say something, but he sat still and held her gaze. She wasn't sure if his silence was a good sign, but he was listening. "So, I made up a new identity and crashed the reunion to meet you." She pinned her arms across her stomach and bit down on her lip. "The rest you know." Feeling faintly ill, she sat back. Her chest closed like a vise around her heart, but she refused to look away. "I'll answer any questions you have before you throw me out."

A muscle tightened along his jaw line. "Is that all I was to you? A way up the ladder?"

"At first." Her voice was barely a whisper.

He leaned closer. "And then?"

"Then, I got to know you." She let out a short sigh. "That's when everything changed."

"But you still wrote lies about me."

Her chest tightened. "You won't believe me, but I

wrote what I did to protect you."

He puffed out a short breath of air. "You're right. I don't believe you."

"I write good copy for the tabloids, so I am well aware of what people think of trash journalism." The disdain on Lance's face told her she'd picked the wrong words. "Okay, maybe it's not exactly *good* writing, but a lot of people can't get enough gossip about famous people."

Lance rocked back in his leather chair but said nothing.

He wasn't making her apology easy, and she could hardly blame him. "My boss is a ruthless man. He cares about the bottom line and not about the truth or who gets hurt. He only wants to make the numbers work." When the dark gaze meeting hers remained impassive, a ripple of panic rushed through her stomach "Yes, I wrote those stories, and yes, they were not entirely factual, but if I didn't turn in copy, my boss would have assigned a major carnivore to cover your campaign. Believe me, his stories would be much worse."

Lance raised an eyebrow. "You could have told me. We could have worked out something."

Kate forced a laugh. "Imagine that. A politician and a reporter on the same side." Her smile quickly faded when Lance did not react. She was trapped in a situation she created and had no idea what to do or what to say next. Lance's expression stayed benign. How could she convince him she was truly sorry for what she did when he wouldn't even give her the slightest hint he cared about anything she said? As tired as she was of her own lies and half-truths, she would have to rehash the whole sordid story.

Her cheeks burned and her throat felt thick, but she had to try. "I started to tell you a few times."

"Why didn't you?"

His voice was flat. She wasn't getting through. "I didn't say anything because I—" She pressed her lips together afraid what she was thinking would turn into words. *Because I fell in love with you and was afraid I'd never see you again once you knew I lied.*

"Because you what?"

"Because I was afraid how you'd react." Guilt gnawed at her soul.

Lance pointed to the file folder. "And playing your game until my reputation is in question is better than the truth?"

Her frustration turned to irritation. "I'm apologizing. Yell. Shout. Threaten to have me arrested or throw me out, but don't just sit there calmly letting me dig myself a deeper hole."

He tipped back his head. "Why should I do any of that?"

"Because most people do something when they are angry, not just sit calmly and let the other person self-destruct."

He shook his head. "Sorry if you think that's what I'm doing. As a senator, I learned not to let emotions get in the way of specifics."

He was right. The tight mouth, glittering eyes, and set jaw did not belong to a man succumbing to verbal anger. "I see that."

He held her gaze. "What do you do when you're angry?"

To dissolve the thick tension surrounding them, Kate hunted for something light and humorous. She grabbed the first thought entering her mind. "I eat a bag of cheese puffs. The crumbs stick to everything, but getting out the orange color is very therapeutic." A stupid thing to say, plus the tactic did not produce the desired effect. Lance's face had not changed.

He stood. "Well, I don't seem to have those handy." He adjusted the buttons on his suit jacket and rang for his intern. She answered on the first ring.

"Yes, sir?"

"Ms. Stapleton is ready to leave." His head lifted. "As I said, I have a committee meeting."

Kate's heart hammered. "Lance, please. I don't want our relationship to end this way." Seeing him round the desk and walk toward her, she froze.

He stopped just as his office door opened and gestured to the way out. "Goodbye, Ms. Stapleton. My assistant will show you the way to the parking lot."

The pain of his stiff goodbye was as sharp as ice splintering in her chest. She slowly stood. Her gaze held Lance's as she walked toward the door. He stepped back as she passed him as though he didn't want any contact, and that's when she knew anything they might have had was really over. Heart breaking, she turned at the door and whispered, "Goodbye, Senator."

His silence cut deep. The ache in her heart became almost unbearable. As she walked out, she could barely breathe. But somehow through the pain and tears that slipped unheeded down her face, she said what she hadn't been able to say and he would never hear.

"I love you."

****

Lance sat on the chair Kate had occupied and stared at the closed office door. Why did he feel so empty? His confusion escalated. Why did he even care?

Kate deliberately deceived him. So why was he holding on to each and every memory they made? He leaned back. Was he insane to think they could salvage anything? His career might survive without her, but would he? The depth of his anger at her ruse was only eclipsed by the emotional tug of remaining feelings.

As hard as it was to look past her deception, that's exactly what his heart told him to do. Though he felt betrayed and empty, he was also heart sore. For a long while he sat, head bent, hands resting on his knees, until the drone of the intercom interrupted his thoughts. He stood and acknowledged the reminder he was already late for his committee meeting.

Bewilderment shivered up his spine as he mulled over the conversation with Kate. Ill equipped for her visit, he acted the fool. She tried to defend herself by laying out the journalistic who-what-when-where-why of her situation, but he refused to acknowledge any of the reasoning she offered. But now, thinking about what she said and why she took the assignment, maybe in some sort of outrageous viewpoint, her rationalization made sense.

When he finally allowed himself to admit things were not finished between them, possibilities jolted him.

Call her.

The words echoed in his head. A myriad of emotions swept through him. Anger. Attraction. Emptiness. He had broken his own rule of involvement, but worse was the stinging ache of loneliness flooding his body.

Call her.

He could no longer fight the need. He began to punch her number on his desk phone then hesitated, unsure of what he could offer. Would a cautious, possibly temporary, relationship be enough to discover if trust could return and bring with it something more? Could he forgive the lies, or did he only crave the feelings that flared between them? How much time did he have to decide between heart and heat? A month? A year? Never? And what political hit would his career take if another tabloid reporter broke an even darker story when the truth came out?

So many questions. So many decisions. What was he willing to let the world know about his personal life so close to an election? Could his constituency accept he fell in love with the tabloid reporter who tried to ruin his career, or would the world think he was merely playing along to protect himself from scandal?

Confusion raged until one question blurred into another, and he could not think straight. One thing did remain clear—before he could speak again to Kate, he had to come to terms with an answer to the ultimate looming question. What did he really want? Duty or desire? At the moment, he didn't think he could have both.

Chapter Fourteen

Back in New Jersey later that evening, Kate learned things about crying she never knew before. By three in the morning, she thought crying oneself to death might very well be possible. She spent the night alternately sobbing and grabbing the tissue box and running to the bathroom to splash cold water on her swollen eyes. By morning, she still did not know what turn the situation she put in motion might take.

She would not write one more trash article for Gartman and didn't really know if she'd have her job much longer anyway. She should have left *The Analytical* months ago, but she'd stay, if she could, until after the election and do everything possible to help Lance.

Warring thoughts swirled inside her head as she drove to the office. Should she go on offense or play defense? She could not decide. She hoped to get to her cubicle unnoticed.

"Hey, Stapleton, great article," one of her colleagues shouted when he saw her.

She gave him a careless wave. "Whatever."

'Gonna give Benson a run for his money," another called out.

Not on the unemployment line. She ignored the rest of the comments and headed for her workspace. Once there, she dropped into the chair, shoved her handbag into the bottom desk drawer, and slammed it shut.

"Rough night?"

Kate glanced up.

Arms folded, Susan stood in the hallway.

"No."

She walked to the desk. "With an entrance like yours, you are not fooling anyone." She cupped Kate's chin and studied her face. "You look like heck."

"Thanks, because that's exactly how I feel." Kate shook her chin free.

"I suspect not from work, but from man trouble," Susan said. "I've been there so I can tell."

Somehow Kate stopped herself from laughing out loud. Man trouble was a weak description of what she instigated. She swallowed the ache rising in her throat when she admitted the pain came from the same place as the love. "I have really screwed up this time."

Susan pulled over a chair and sat. "Tell Mama what happened, and we'll fix it together."

"You can't fix this." She shook her head and stared down at her hands.

"You and Senator McDreamy have a lover's quarrel?"

"Worse."

"How much worse?"

Kate looked at Susan and uttered the two words that ended everything. "He knows." For the next hour, Kate told Susan the whole sordid story.

Susan offered nothing just wished her luck and hightailed out of the cubicle.

Kate hadn't expected Gandhi-like solutions from her friend, but a few suggestions would have been nice. Before confronting Gartman, she checked the current social media reaction to the last article *The Analytical* ran about Lance. She hoped the furor died down without too much damage done, but when she logged on, a breaking news story filled every mainstream media site. Something big was happening.

As the camera shot zoomed to a reporter pointing to law enforcement in action behind him, she leaned forward and turned up the volume. Blue and red lights flashed lighting the scene like lasers. The shot shifted to focus on a sheriff K-9 officer and police dog exiting a specially-equipped cruiser. The camera followed the officer and the police dog to the building housing Lance's campaign headquarters.

"...to recap, this morning the County Sheriff's Office received a tip of a possible drug deal going down inside the campaign office of Senator Lance Michaels. Sheriff's Officers plus officers from the local police department along with federal DEA officials cleared the building. The senator's campaign staff has been removed while the office is searched by the County K-9 unit. Senator Michaels is voluntarily on his way to New Jersey from Washington and will be questioned by local authorities once he arrives. Stay tuned to this station for further updates."

For a few moments, Kate felt as though she'd been shell-shocked. When the white noise cleared, slowly her thoughts gelled with a dreadful supposition. Gartman did this. "Susan! I need you." Kate felt the world slowed to slow motion as she watched the story unfold. "Now, Susan."

Susan came running. "What is it?"

Kate pointed to the laptop.

She circled the desk and looked from the computer

screen to Kate. "Your face is as gray as the tile floor. What is going on?"

Kate slumped in the chair as though someone landed a blow to her chest. "The police are searching Lance's campaign office." She gritted her teeth. "For possible drugs, no less."

Susan stared at the screen. "I count eight police cruisers from four different departments all lit like Christmas lights."

Kate cocked her head and narrowed her eyes. "I smell a rat named Gartman."

Susan's eyebrows drew down. "Do you really think he's involved somehow?"

"This situation has his fingerprints all over it." Kate bared her teeth. "I'd bet a year's salary he wasn't satisfied with the speed in which he was ruining Lance's career, so he stirred the pot." She clenched her jaw so hard the pain radiated to her eyes. "He's done that before."

"He's definitely a slime ball." Susan wrinkled her nose.

Kate nodded. "Lance told me he lost a cousin to drugs and was trying to move Congress toward taking a more pro-active role dealing with the opioid crisis." She shook her head. "I might have mentioned it to Gartman in frustration when I was defending Lance."

"No!" Susan widened her eyes. "So, you really think the raid was set up."

"I know Lance. He's doing all he can to battle the drug crisis." She carved a hand through her hair, grabbing the back of her head as she watched more footage. She punched a fist in the air. "This is disgusting."

"I'll give you Gartman's a pig, but he's smart enough not to tangle with the feds for a story." She folded her arms across her chest. "Are you sure he'd stoop that low?"

Kate thought for a moment and then spit out a pent-up breath. "Maybe not but Benson would."

****

Greeted by the media camped on the sidewalk outside the County Prosecutors Office, Lance arrived in time to be live on the early evening news. With microphones and cameras pointed at him while the reporters barked questions about drugs and his reputation until their voices sounded like one big ear-splitting sound, he kept his gaze forward as he walked toward the door.

With arms spread, Jack cleared a way through the pressing mob. "Senator Michaels will answer all your questions after he speaks with authorities." He swiped at a camera getting too close as he and Lance moved toward the building. With the help of local PD, he barely closed the door on the crush of reporters clamoring for a comment. "Brutal, sir," he said once inside.

Lance nodded. His thoughts scrambled to comprehend what was happening. He ran a hand through his hair. "I don't understand this."

"Someone obviously made a mistake," Jack said. "Do you think Ms. Stapleton had something to do with this operation? After all, she is a tabloid reporter."

A sour tang rose in Lance's mouth. "No, I don't. Stories are one thing, but a raid by law enforcement is a lot more serious." Hands on hips, he stared at the front door and watched the reporters outside swell forward

210

when they saw his silhouette in the beveled glass. He stepped back and pointed to the lettering on the door. "My face surrounded by the words 'County Prosecutor's Office' would be a great lead shot for the late evening news."

Jack nodded but said nothing.

At security, Lance placed his watch, wallet, and phone in the tray provided by the Sheriff's Officer manning the security metal detector and walked to the other side without incident. He scooped the articles from the tray as it rolled from the scanner.

Jack cleared security right behind.

"Down the hall to the right," the Sheriff's Officer said.

Lance nodded. At another security point at the end of the hall, the tinny sound of an intercom announced someone would be with them shortly. He took three steps away.

"I'm sure this misunderstanding will be all cleared soon," Jack said.

"Maybe, but no one in the media is reporting anything positive right now. Ratings first, and then a retraction." Lance snickered. "Positioned at the end of the broadcast right before the closing credits." He heard the door open and turned.

An expressionless DEA agent approached. "Thank you for coming, Senator." He extended a hand. "Don Brown."

Lance took the hand offered and gestured to Jack. "And this is the head of my security staff, Jack Turner."

Jack and the agent exchanged a perfunctory nod.

"I want to clear this misunderstanding as quickly as possible," Lance said.

"For that, I need to ask a few questions." He gestured toward the door. "This way, Senator."

Jack started to follow but was quickly stopped by the agent's raised hand. "Mr. Turner, we'll be speaking to Senator Michaels alone."

Lance saw a puzzled look cross Jack's face as he looked from the agent. "Get some coffee, Jack. It was a long ride from D.C. I'm sure this is strictly standard procedure."

Jack glanced at the agent who did not confirm nor deny the statement.

"Agent Brown, can you have someone show Jack another way out? I would prefer the media didn't mob him."

"Of course." The agent gestured to the receptionist sitting at the desk to the right. "Please have someone direct Mr. Turner to the rear entrance."

"Certainly, sir," she replied

Lance turned to Jack. "I'll call you when I'm through here."

"An hour? Two maybe?" Jack asked.

"You might want to get dinner with that coffee," the agent answered.

Lance lifted a single eyebrow. This matter was much worse than he thought.

****

Kate shoved Gartman's office door so hard it hit the wall. She stormed inside like a banshee on a mission. "What have you done?"

Gartman watched the news unfold on a small television on his desk.

With a smirk and arms folded across his chest, Benson stood next to him. "You should knock when you enter an office. Far more professional, Kate."

She pointed a shaky finger at Benson. "You. Out!"

Benson's gaze flickered. "This is not your office."

Gartman lifted his chin. "Close the door on your way out, Benson."

Making no effort to move, Benson's mouth flew open, and he glared at his boss.

"Now." Gartman flicked his hand toward the hall.

With a huff, Benson left.

Kate glared and pointed to the TV. "You did this, didn't you?"

He shrugged. "Does it matter?"

"Of course, it matters. What I don't know is how you got so many agencies involved so quickly."

Gartman laughed. "Let's just say a well-placed suggestion in the right ear turned the tide."

Kate stepped forward like a knight ready for the battle. "Benson." Saying his name made the anger inside her bubble like a volcano preparing to erupt.

"He still maintains a few contacts in law enforcement."

Her eyes narrowed. "From a failed attempt to make it through the county police academy."

"Who cares? Fact is, *The Analytical* has been mentioned on every mainstream news channel as breaking this story. Subscriptions are going through the roof."

A large knot lodged in her throat. Anything she said would fall on deaf ears. She could not compete with money and notoriety. "Is that all you care about?"

Gartman lifted his shoulders. "Pays the rent."

Her cheeks burned. That's what she said to Lance when she tried to make him understand why she took a job with the tabloid. The words sounded hollow, and she finally understood.

"What about the truth?" Her pulse raced, and her heart pounded. "Lance does not have anything to do with drugs. In fact, he is intent on calling attention to the overuse of prescription drugs." Over Gartman's shoulder, she watched the K-9 Unit exit the campaign office. Her stomach clenched, trying to contain the swirling feeling of nausea. She shot Gartman a stinging look. "He might not recover from this scandal."

Gartman swiped a hand in front of his face. "Politicians always have a scandal or two. Generally, they come out fine."

Rage overcame her blistering dread. She picked up Gartman's cell phone from the desktop and held it out. "You need to fix this."

He took it and dropped the phone back on the desktop. "One way or another, this topic will work itself out in a few days."

When she realized he was serious about not helping, despair rolled over her. *How could Lance ever think about forgiving her now?*

Gartman resumed watching the news. He sat back and folded his arms over his chest. "Will you look at that? It didn't take long for Senator Michaels' opponent to get his mug on camera. Network news is getting a quote now, and he's thanking *The Analytical* for bringing this bombshell to light."

As she listened to Lance's challenger extol *The Analytical* and condemn Lance for his deception, Kate's ire overcame her anguish. She reached over and shut off the TV.

Gartman rose and set his jaw. "Now look here,

missy—"

She stood in front of him. "No, you look here." She pointed to her face. "Because this is the last time you'll be seeing me in this office. But before I go, you will listen." She stepped closer and nearly laughed when Gartman fell backwards into his desk chair. She grabbed the armrests and trapped him. "You put Lance in a horrible position, and you need to get him out. He'll have to spend days, maybe weeks, clearing his name. This fiasco could cost him the election. He does not deserve the treatment the press is giving him right now, and you know it. If you aren't making the call to tell the mainstream media the truth, I'll do it." She grabbed his phone from the desktop and slipped it down her shirt, thankful her bra stopped the phone from sliding out.

Gartman surged forward.

Kate moved back.

"Just try to get your phone back," she challenged. "I don't think you want that story on the air."

His face paled. "What are you doing with my cell?"

She didn't really know why she grabbed his phone, but she did know now was her turn to bluff. "I'll be giving your phone to a teckie friend. If anything is in memory to prove you orchestrated this farce, he'll find it." From the expression on Gartman's ashen face, she knew he was not sure the phone was entirely clean. Momentarily, she had the upper hand.

"You realize your actions might close this place. That means no job."

She laughed. "I don't have one now."

****

Late evening Lance called Jack to say he was on his way to Lawrenceville and would meet him there. He'd been at the Prosecutor's office for over six hours before he was suddenly allowed to leave. After going over the facts what seemed like a hundred times, he was tired and in no mood to speak to the press or drive back to D.C.

He turned onto his street and was surprised to see no network vans with roof mounted cameras nor reporters waiting to pounce surrounding his childhood home. He doubted being at the right house. In the driveway, he lowered the driver side window, sat in the darkening light, and listened. The last of the crickets navigated the nighttime dating scene with their chirping. As a boy, the sound was quite annoying and kept him awake, but now he preferred it over the monotone commotion of rapid-fire questions hurled by the persistent detectives in a small room he'd occupied for hours.

After a few minutes, he remotely opened the garage door and pulled the car inside. Three steps later, he was inside his home where, for the first time all day, he felt safe. He slid the keys across the kitchen table and dropped onto one of the oak stools at the island.

Jack walked in and caught the keys before they dropped off the table edge. "If you lose these, we'll have to walk to D.C."

Lance didn't look up. "I'll be here for a few days. I need to go to the campaign office in the morning and apologize to whatever staff hasn't walked out on me."

"I don't think any will," Jack replied. "I want to turn on the news and get an update." He gestured to the living room. "Coming?"

Lance shook his head. "I've had enough in-depth for one day."

Jack disappeared around the corner. A few minutes later, he rushed back and pulled Lance by an arm from the stool. "You have to see this."

"No. I don't." Lance freed himself. "I need some quiet time to sort out what happened today and think how I can salvage the campaign."

"I promise after you see what's happening, you won't be worried."

"How?" Lance's brow furrowed.

A smile broke across Jack's face. "Your girlfriend is on TV with a whole mess of mikes in her face telling the world her boss set up the raid with a false tip. Apparently, she has turned over credible proof to the prosecutor to back her story."

Lance jumped to his feet. His eyes widened. "She what?" He elbowed past Jack and headed for the living room.

"So, she *is* your girlfriend then?" Jack called out.

Lance disappeared down the hallway toward the living room. "Maybe," Lance's fading voice answered. "Just maybe."

Chapter Fifteen

Outside Kate's house, a car horn sounded followed by relentless pounding on her front door. According to the luminous markings on her watch the time was one a.m. She was both exhausted and annoyed. *Why won't they leave me alone?*

She'd told her story to what seemed like a hundred reporters and was sure she had not missed any network, news source, or online media dump. The irony hit her, and she laughed out loud. A hundred reporters. No wonder she couldn't get a real job. Every news bureau was over staffed.

She waited for an instant then slipped flip-flops onto her feet and walked toward the door. She grabbed the door knob, looked at the floor, and sighed. Probably a stringer hoping for the big break just like she had been when she first started writing. She'd give him or her an exclusive and advice not to get personally involved in the story. But not tonight. She just couldn't rehash what she had done again. The wound was still very raw. Lordy, she hated being on the wrong end of a news story. For the first time, she genuinely realized the consequences of a callous press.

With downcast eyes, she yanked open the door. "No more interviews today."

"I don't want an interview, Kate."

As though sprayed with liquid nitrogen, she froze.

She looked up. "Lance. What are you doing here?"

He held her gaze. "I saw the news."

When warmth returned to her body, Kate's first instinct was to drag him inside so a reporter—worse, maybe even Gartman or Benson—couldn't take a long-range camera shot and throw suspicion into her confession that cleared his name. Her second instinct was to throw her arms around him and kiss him silly.

Afraid to make the wrong choice, she simply stood still and anxiously scanned his features. "You probably don't want to hear this, but I really think you need to come inside before you and I are front page news." She opened the door wider and took a small step to one side before looking past him and scanning the street. Aside from a dog walking in the neighbor's front yard, nothing seemed out of place. Confusion rose. She couldn't imagine the media giving up so soon.

"No one is coming." Lance stepped inside.

She closed the door. His expression gave little away. "How do you know?"

"Because Gartman has been taken to the Prosecutor's Office for questioning, and the media is camped out there waiting for an official update from the authorities. My sources say he will be charged with making false statements to law enforcement."

Kate looked at his smile and burst into tears.

Lance pulled her against him.

His arms encircled her as she cried against his neck. "I'm sorry. I'm so sorry. I am an awful person." Between sobs, she looked into his eyes, and the flash of understanding she saw made her feel as though bird's wings beat against her belly.

He stepped back and released her. "We need to

talk."

"We did. In Washington."

"More needs to be said."

Was he here to say the final goodbye? Sighing, she shook her head. "You need to put this mess behind you and concentrate on your re-election. I'd just be a daily reminder. Maybe you should go."

"You asked me in." He took her hand. "I can't imagine the invitation was just out of fear of pictures posted on a social media site."

"It wasn't," she whispered.

They walked to the living room and sat side-by-side on the sofa. "You were pretty fearless today."

Kate almost smiled. "Getting out the truth was the right thing to do. I couldn't live with myself if lies destroyed your career in the senate. You're a good man, Senator Michaels. You deserve to have a chance to change the world."

"What about you?"

Regret fisted in her stomach alongside the guilt. Her heart ached at the thought of a few states permanently separating them after the election, but the best thing would be for her to stay away. "I don't think I'll be looking for work from any news media any time soon. What news source will want a reputation-damaged reporter?" She snickered. "But I know I can be a darn good greeter at one of those big-box stores."

Lance grinned. "Or you could really sell Johnny ads."

"You know I made up that career choice, too," she admitted.

"Apparently."

"Hey." She slapped her hands together. "I'm a

really good fiction writer. Maybe I can do the great American novel."

"You could." He took his forefinger and moved a lock of hair behind her ear.

Her eyes slowly filled with tears. "I screwed up pretty badly."

He nodded. "You did. But you bared your soul on national television for me without any hesitation or thought of the consequences. No one in Washington would ever do that."

She tipped her head. "Guess I won't look for a job there then."

He ran the back of a hand down her cheek. "I've never met anyone quite like you."

"Bet you're happy you haven't." She sniffed and wiped a tear trickling down her cheek with the back of her hand.

They stared at each other for long moment, and in that span of time, Kate saw the arc of their relationship—the way it began and the way it eroded. Maybe if she confessed sooner, they'd have a chance, but now she could not see a way to save what might have been. As her mind replayed all her mistakes, time seemed to spin out of control. Her head pounded with the thoughts of all the missed opportunities.

She stood. "I suppose you need to get somewhere to do something." She gave him a weak smile. "But I'm glad you came."

Lance rose and took her hands in his. "I am, too." He looked at their entwined fingers and then into her eyes. "Before I go, I have a question, and I'd like a straightforward, honest answer."

She nodded. "Ask away. Seems I'm on an honesty

roll."

"What about us?"

"Us?" she asked in a small voice. "Is there an us?"

"I'll let you decide."

Tears again welled in her eyes. "How can you ever trust me?"

He released her hands and tipped her chin with his fingertips. "I can because I love you."

I love you. The words seeped into her soul unfurling warmth within her chest. He loved her even after what she had done, after she almost ruined his political career. The tears broke free, and her breath expelled in a rush of air. "I love you, too."

"Good. At least we finally agree on something."

Wild and celebratory, he whirled in a circle as his mouth crushed hers. When they stopped, he slid her back down the front of him with deliberate slowness, caressing her back and ribs.

The back door suddenly creaked open, and they both looked toward the sound.

"I hope a reporter isn't sneaking in to get a scoop," Kate said.

"It's not."

Lance grinned, dimples winking at her. "What's going on?"

A moment later, Jack turned the corner, his arms full of groceries. He set down the bags, crossed his arms over his chest, and leaned against the archway. "Well, well, well," he drawled. "What do we have here?"

Lance craned his neck around Kate and looked at Jack.

Kate kept her arms around Lance's neck, unwilling

to let him go despite the interruption.

"What we have here," Lance answered, "is Kate Stapleton, the woman who made my life pure hell lately."

"Is she joining the campaign team?" Jack asked with a wink.

Lance grinned. "What do you say, Kate? Want to join the Michaels for Senate team?"

She kissed him with a loud smack. "Depends on you."

Lance pulled her closer. "I say sign her up." He looked at Jack. "Did you get what I asked?"

Jack nodded. "Right here in the hallway."

"Then bye." Lance shooed him away.

Jack pulled his shoulder from the doorway. "I see I'm not needed. Might as well check on campaign headquarters and let anyone there know all is well." He saluted and walked away. A minute later, his car started. The fading sound of the engine gave way to silence.

Alone now, Kate looked into Lance's eyes. "I can't believe you came here."

"The last few days were awful. I couldn't concentrate. I thought of nothing but you. That's when I knew we had some unfinished business. The way I acted when you came to Washington was unforgiveable, and I was afraid I'd lost you."

Relief swept her. "I was scared, too."

Lance nuzzled her neck. "Another thing we share."

She saw things clearly now. Nothing was as important as this moment. She snuggled into the curve of his arm. "I felt an instant attraction to you the night of the reunion. Each time I was with you, the pull became stronger, and it terrified me. I thought you were the consummate politician, and politicians always seem so insincere. Then I got to know you, and I realized I was falling in love." She rested her forehead on his. "Can we do this? Are you sure you won't doubt me after what I did?"

"Never. You exposed yourself on national television to save me. If that wasn't the ultimate act of love and sacrifice, I don't know what is."

"I promise I will never lie to you again."

When he smiled, his eyes crinkled at the corners, and Kate knew she'd never get tired of counting the tiny lines if they lived to be a hundred.

His smile widened. "I know you won't." His thumb caressed her lips before he gently erased the space between their mouths and kissed her. After a few more kisses, he gently broke contact. "I have something for you." He walked to the hallway and picked up the grocery bags Jack left on the floor. He pointed toward the sofa. "Sit."

She complied.

He moved a footstool in front of her and, with a flourish, dumped the contents of the bags onto it.

Kate took one look and burst out laughing.

"Cheese snacks," Lance proudly announced. "You said you eat them when you were upset. I wasn't taking any chances."

Kate ripped open a bag and grabbed a handful of the orange snack sticks. "And now, I eat them when I'm happy."

Lance sat beside her. "I guess I do, too." He rested a hand on her cheek. "I love you, Kate. We can do this."

"I love you, too," she whispered. "But are you sure?"

"I can't promise life in Washington will be easy, but I can promise it will be an adventure."

"Then I'm in, and I hope you like orange because I intend to eat a bunch of these every day." She popped a handful of the snacks into her mouth. When he mirrored her move, she knew everything would be just fine.

****

Kate and Lance chose a Friday evening after he was sworn into office for a second term for their wedding. Kate wore a short, white dress with elbow-length sleeves, and Lance wore the same suit as when he met her. White roses and lilacs, flowers reminding her of both grandmothers, made up her bouquet.

Only those they loved most attended the outdoor ceremony in the White House Rose Garden, among them their parents, Jack, Susan and a few close friends. Her father walked her across the lawn to a flower-covered arch where Lance and a minister waited.

Lance shook her father's hand. "Mr. Stapleton, I promise to love your daughter and keep her safe."

"And give her mother and I some grandchildren," her father added. He kissed Kate on the cheek and moved to his seat.

"Yes, sir." Lance took Kate's hand and winked. "Ready?"

So much had stood between them, but they still fell in love. Kate was sure nothing else would ever stand in their way. She nodded. "So ready."

The service lasted only about seven minutes. When the minister told Lance he could kiss his bride, Lance obliged with a flourish that nearly bent Kate in two.

When she righted, she closed her arms around his neck. His skin smelled of the musky aftershave she knew so well. She slipped her fingers into his hair and cradled his head. "Mrs. Lance Michaels," she whispered. "I can hardly believe it."

"From now until forever." He laughed. "But for the present, I do believe your father put in a rather tall order. One we need to start delivering as soon as possible." He grimaced. "But I see a small problem."

Kate raised her right hand. "I swear I didn't have anything to do with that."

"Neither did I." Lance winked. "Yet."

Kate laughed. "Explain."

"Last night I got a call from party leadership. My name is actually being bantered around for a higher office."

Kate's eyes widened. "I guess I better dive into learning protocols." She shrugged. "But we do have six years."

"Four," Lance corrected. "That particular campaign starts early and lasts about two years."

"What's higher than senator?" As she realized what was being proposed, she couldn't keep her mouth from falling open. "You mean?"

He nodded. "You up for the challenge?"

"You bet I am." Kate raised and lowered her eyebrows. "And there's nothing cuter than a wholesome family campaign photo."

"Really?"

"I've wanted to be a mom since I got my first doll." She looked into his eyes. "Here in Washington or in a condo in Jersey, a family with you is more than I ever dreamed possible lately."

"How about in a big white house on Pennsylvania Avenue?"

She held up a palm to stop him. She never pictured getting married to anyone of note, but she just had so why not go for the gold? She tilted her head. "Can I redecorate?"

"To a degree."

She laughed out loud. "The press will not be kind to my fashion choices."

Lance tossed his head. "You care?"

"No." She thought for a moment, and her smile grew. "It could be fun." She pretended to ponder her decision. She placed her hands on his forearms and squeezed. "I am so in."

He stared for an extended amount of time. "You sure?"

"Totally."

His kiss was filled with the promise he'd never leave her and would always be by her side ready to help her deal with the uncertainty of life in Washington politics.

As they came up for air, Kate cupped his cheek. "We have time for two children to be in those campaign photos if we get started right away."

His smile matched hers. "To quote the woman I love, 'I am so in.' Let's go."

A word about the author...

Born long ago in a place not so far away, Shenandoah, Pennsylvania, Kathryn Quick has been writing since the Sisters in St. Casmir's Grammar School gave her the ruled yellow paper and a number two pencil. She writes contemporary romances, romantic comedies, and historical romances, as well as urban fantasy.

A former member of New Jersey Romance Writers (NJRW President 1992 and 2001) and a member of Romance Writers of America, she is one of the founding members of Liberty States Fiction Writers, a multi-genre writers' organization dedicated to furthering the craft of writing and helping aspiring writers move on to publication.

While writing romances has been her dream for many years, the book of Kathye's heart is a nonfiction work, still in concept, entitled *Hi, Mom and Dad, How Are Things in Heaven*, developed after the death of her mother and tweaked to add the passing of her father. The book deals with coping with grief though humor.

Kathye also writes as P. K. Eden with colleague, Patt Mahailoff. *Firebrand*, their debut urban fantasy, has been heralded for having lush worlds and colorful characters full of secrets and magic. Based on the fall of the Garden of Eden, *Firebrand* has won two Reviewer's Choice Awards.

Kathye originally wanted to be President of the United States or an organic chemist, but somehow life got in the way. She married right out of high school and had a set of twins two years later. The Presidency seemed out of reach, and night school to get her Ph.D.

to create a new molecule that would ultimately result in the betterment of humankind seemed a little time-consuming while trying to raise twins, so she decided to write instead.

Kathye is married to her real-life hero Donald and has three grown sons all having adventures of their own. She is a die-hard New Jersey Devils fan and works for Somerset County government (as close as she could get to the White House) and is plotting a novel about a new molecule that will ultimately result in the betterment of humankind.

www.kathrynquick.com

~

Other Titles by the Author
Cynthia and Constantine
In the "Bachelors Three" series
Bachelor.com
Solid Gold Bachelor

Thank you for purchasing
this publication of The Wild Rose Press, Inc.

For questions or more information
contact us at
info@thewildrosepress.com.

The Wild Rose Press, Inc.
www.thewildrosepress.com

www.ingramcontent.com/pod-product-compliance
Lightning Source LLC
Chambersburg PA
CBHW070443260626
47161CB00004B/1186